Tombstone Travesty:
Allie Earp Remembers

Tombstone Travesty:
Allie Earp Remembers

A Western Story

Jane Candia Coleman

Five Star • Waterville, Maine

First Edition
First Printing: December 2004

Published in 2004 in conjunction with
Golden West Literary Agency

Set in 11 pt. Plantin by Elena Picard.

Printed in the United States on permanent paper.

Library of Congress Cataloging-in-Publication Data

Coleman, Jane Candia.
   Tombstone travesty : Allie Earp remembers : a western
story / by Jane Candia Coleman.—1st ed.
       p. cm.
     ISBN 1-59414-011-1 (hc : alk. paper)
     1. Earp, Allie, 1848 or 9–1947—Fiction. 2. Earp, Virgil,
d. 1905—Fiction. 3. Tombstone (Ariz.)—Fiction.
4. Women pioneers—Fiction. I. Title.
PS3553.O47427T66 2004
813'.54—dc22   2004057955

To "Aunt Allie" Earp
who deserves her real story told.

Prologue

I've never been able to keep my mouth shut or stop from cussing, either. It's a good thing Virge didn't mind. He always just laughed and egged me on, saying I was no bigger than a 'skeeter, but my bite was ten times worse. So when this writer fella who's been coming here, pumping me for what I remember and bringing me little presents—snuff, cause he knows I have a weakness for it, and sometimes whiskey to get me going—when he came in this morning to show me the book he wrote, I let him have it with both barrels, I was that mad.

"Why you little, no-'count son-of-a-bitch!" I was yelling loud as I could. "I'll kill you if you ever publish any of this bullshit you made up about us Earps."

He believed me. I might be old, but I ain't feeble. And I can shoot as good as I always did.

"I . . . I . . . I . . . ," was all he could get out.

"You . . . you . . . you," I mocked him, the lying little hypocrite. "You get out of this house or I'll shoot you right here and be damned to the rug."

He got, all right, slamming the door so hard the windows shook, and I stood there laughing. And hurting. Times like this I miss Virge so bad it hurts like my bones are broken. Times like this I remember the good things and how it was being a part of that family, how it was having a home again even with all the troubles.

Yes, I remember plain as day. All of it, good and bad, sorrowful and sweet as the scent of prairie flowers on a spring wind.

Chapter One

Wyatt, Sadie, Virge, and me were sitting around the camp-fire after supper, and Tombstone seemed as far away as Los Angeles. But we carried the memory of that place with us all the time—the violence, the lies, Morg's death, and Virge's crippled arm. He hated being a cripple, but he'd learned to live with it just like I learned to put up with his anger. That's what a wife does—keep going, hide her feelings from her man, and always looking over her shoulder in case the past shows up—armed.

I figured going out to the desert to hunt for gold was Wyatt's way of putting Tombstone behind him. No ghosts out there, no old enemies hiding in ambush, only the quiet, the shadows of big mesquites and ironwood trees, the sun's last light on the Colorado River, and out in the brush a couple of coyotes hunting.

Sadie? Well, I never could figure her. She loved the desert same as Wyatt, but I thought she came along on his treasure hunts because she wanted a gold mine of her own, and because she always kept an eye on Wyatt in case he got an idea to stray. After all, he'd left Mattie for her, and he always had an eye for the ladies, so how could she tell when he'd do it again? If her conscience pricked her over Mattie, though, she'd have died before admitting it. She was a proud one, and tough. Had to be just like the rest of us Earp women. You married an Earp, you took the good along with the bad, and there was more than enough bad to go around. Seemed like trouble followed all of us all the time except out there on the Mojave Desert with night coming on and a little horned moon painted on the sky.

Maybe it was because I was remembering Tombstone that Sadie started talking about it. I tried not to listen because going over the past ain't a cure for the present. She threw a log on the fire, and it blazed up and shone on her face—the same face that started all our trouble—and she said: "Maybe tomorrow we'll get lucky. Maybe tomorrow we'll strike it rich. I've got a feeling about this place. There are lucky spots. We just haven't found one." She frowned, and her eyes caught the fire like a mirror. "There's places that have a curse on them. Like Tombstone. Evil came up out of the ground and infected everybody, and there was no getting away from it. Even out here it's like that evil's still with us."

She'd put her finger on the trouble, but I wondered what she'd have said about Ponca Bottom where I was born. That country along the Missouri had a power, too, but it was a power that came from good, a kind of magic that I recognized even as a kid. A magic that couldn't be got rid of even when the Border Wars started and kept us all on edge day and night. Especially at night with the sound of horses passing, and the riders up to no good. We lived through seven years of fighting before Pa went off with the First Nebraska to fight for the Union. He never came back, but by that time I was old enough, had seen enough to know that magic doesn't help you through the bad times. You got to help yourself as best you can or get tromped on. Nobody's ever tromped on me. Tromp on Allie Sullivan Earp and get bit afore you know it.

"Allie's tongue can cut rope," Mum always said, but when you're little and a female to boot, you got to find some way to win. I've been mean when I had to and stubborn as a goat. I've cussed and hit out at whoever needed it and never been sorry.

Why'd Sadie have to talk about it? I wondered. *Why'd she go and bring the old trouble into our peace?* Maybe I was getting old, or maybe I figured I'd save my ammunition for a better time. Whatever, I kept quiet, got up, and walked out to where the horses was hobbled, where the Injun, Dude, who always camped with Wyatt sort of like a bodyguard, sat with his back against an ironwood. He was some kind of California Injun, not like the ones I grew up with in Nebraska, but like any Injun he understood a person's need for a little privacy. He nodded when I passed, but all he said was: "Don't get lost."

Well, hell, I never been lost in my life! "I can find my way good as any Injun," I told him, and kept on walking till I'd left them all behind. Them and any thoughts of that place that had marked us.

Ponca Bottom. Funny how my mind turned back the years. How I could almost see it—our cabin, and Pa in the cornfield, plowing, and all around the fruits of the earth there for the picking—wild plums, blackberries so sweet they was like honey, and in the fall enough nuts to last us all winter. Back then, it seemed I could make time stand still just by holding my breath, closing my eyes, and making a wish. Usually I wished the same thing. That nothing would ever change, that we could all stay just like we were—Mum and Pa, Melissa, Lydia, Frank, Mary, and me—in what I believed was the same as the paradise told about in the Bible.

I was too young to know that nothing ever stays the same, that sooner or later the world finds you. I was four, maybe five, when the Kansas-Nebraska Act brought trouble right to our doorstep. All of a sudden there was death in the air and folks shouting words I didn't understand—Abolition, state's rights, slavery—and Mum kept the shotgun by the door when Pa was out in the field. We didn't get the shooting and hanging Kansas did, but wagons headed there went through Omaha, some even through our pasture, and always there was night riders up to no good.

"It'll come to war," Pa said one night when we was at supper. The light in the lamp flickered when he spoke, and all of a sudden he looked old.

It scared me. Like I was seeing the future, seeing change, and helpless to stop it.

Mum sighed. "Seems it's already war here. All these folks coming and ready to fight. What'll happen to us?"

"I don't know. I wish I did. But the day anybody brings slaves to Nebraska is the day I start my own fight."

"What's slaves?" I asked, although us kids weren't supposed to interrupt our parents.

Pa stared across the table at me. "It's one man ownin' another. Or a lot of others. And it's wrong."

I thought about that. "Like we own Sally?" Sally was our cow.

"You might say that. 'Cept men ain't animals, and Sally's treated better than some of the slaves I heard about."

By the time us kids crawled into bed, my five-year-old mind was running off in all directions. "I don't want nobody ownin' me," I whispered to Melissa.

She giggled. "You will one day. When you're grown."

"I won't, either." Growing up to me meant trouble.

"Anyhow"—she gave a big yawn—"folks like us ain't slaves, and we sure don't own any. Now go to sleep."

"What if there's a war? Will we get to fight, too?"

"It's men who do the fightin'. Women stay home and worry."

"I bet I could fight good as a man," I said. "Even if I am a girl."

"And if you don't hush talkin', you'll be a sorry one." She turned over, her back to me.

"You ain't my boss," I mumbled, but she didn't answer, and I lay there, hearing all the night sounds—Pa snoring on the other side of the quilt that divided the rooms, the wind in the leaves of the big cottonwood, an owl calling from the creek bottom.

One thing I knew for sure. I didn't want anybody bossing me. Not then, not ever. What I didn't understand was that, when you love somebody, there's no question of who owns who or who gives orders.

That's what I was thinking when Virge found me later that night, a long ways from camp. My feet had taken me up the big wash to where the hills turned rocky, and the trees thinned out.

"I thought you'd got lost." He put his good arm around me, and I leaned up against him.

"Lost!" I said. "All you men can think of is a woman who can't find her way in the dark. I was just rememberin' back."

He shook his head. "Seems we never stop talking about that place. We're marked. Like Cain. I wish we'd never left the farm. Or stayed in Prescott. Had a family instead of followin' some pipe dream." He sounded bone-tired.

"Spilt milk," I told him.

"I'm not cryin'."

"I know that."

13

The Earp men didn't waste time on tears. That was left to us women, but, if we cried, we did it alone where no one could see. The faces we showed were masks, but I reckon everybody does that—hide behind a smile or a pokerface. You're safest that way.

I put my arm around Virge's waist. "Let's go on back. Let's go to bed."

His laugh began down low. I could feel it moving up into his chest. "You got somethin' in mind, Allie?"

"How'd you guess?"

The laugh spilled out, big and jolly, Virge's laugh. "Because I know you down to your toes."

And that's a comfort. Being understood and no need to play games. But being me, I had to have the last word. "That's what you think," I said.

Chapter Two

After the Kansas-Nebraska Act got passed, wagons full of Abolitionists came like a line of ants, one following another till there was roads where there'd only been brush and trees, and noise where there'd been the quiet of empty country. Some of those wagons was filled with new Sharps rifles, although you wouldn't know to look. Pa said they were in boxes marked Bibles. After a while, folks got wise and started calling 'em Beecher's Bibles, after some big preacher back East who was behind buying 'em.

Old Jim Lane and Jim Hickok led a lot of those trains that came past. They couldn't get into Kansas 'cause there was a blockade on the river, and the fighting down there was fierce. So Lane and Hickok figured to sneak the Abolitionists in through the back door, so to say. Many a night there was wagons full of people camped down by the creek, and I sneaked away as much as I could, 'cause it was an education just listening to 'em. Why, some of those men shouted better than a good preacher, but what they said was always the same. Down with slavery! Every man has the right to life and liberty!

Well, I sure agreed with that, and so did Pa, who was usually down there with 'em, although he never was one to get up and talk. Mum always said that's why he'd settled where he did, where there was nobody to bother him when he was thinking.

But those wagons brought the news quicker than the mail, and that was how we heard about the man called John Brown and his sons, raids on places in Kansas we never knew was there, and about the blockade on the river that was bringing half the world into our back yard.

There was wagons headed West, too, to California and Oregon, and I wondered what it'd be like living in a house on wheels, moving every day, leaving a whole life far behind. Well, I found out years later, and I can't say I didn't like it, 'cause I did. But that's getting ahead of myself. That happened after I met Virge and my life changed forever.

In those years there was always kids my age to talk to—neighbor kids and those I never saw again, but we made friends anyhow, played games, skipped stones in the creek, stuffed our faces with whatever fruit was ripe. I remember one little girl—Sarah was her name. She had long blonde curls and a real doll with a china face and a ruffled dress. I wanted that doll, wanted to touch and hold her. All I'd ever had was rag babies or corncobs with faces scratched in 'em and scraps for clothes.

"Can I hold her?" I asked, wanting to so bad my voice came out in a squeak.

Sarah shook her head. "You'll get her dirty."

I didn't understand. "I'll be careful."

She hugged the little doll closer. "No, you won't. I can tell by lookin' at you."

What could she tell? I looked down at myself—bare, muddy feet, Melissa's old skirt dragging at my ankles, my arms a mess of scratches from berry picking, and I purely hated that girl.

I grabbed the doll and ran, and I could run. I headed

straight for the creek where there was an old log laid across. In the middle of it I stopped, my toes digging into the damp wood for a good grip.

"Come get her! Dare you!"

"Snot!" She stood there mad as a mess of yellow jackets.

"Takes one to know one." I backed up slow, feeling my way, and grinned when she started across, wobbling in her fancy lace-up boots, her arms stuck out for balance.

"I'll tell," she hissed just like a snake. "I'll tell and you'll get a whuppin'."

"Nobody whups me." That was a lie, and we both knew it.

"Liar, liar, house on fire," she sang, and that was the last thing she got out before she slipped and fell into the water.

For a minute I thought she was drowning, and it was my fault. No matter what, I hadn't meant anything except to tease and to hold that doll. I tossed it on the bank and jumped in after her, was just hauling her out, her hollering like she was killed, when Jim Hickok came by on that gray horse he always rode.

"Here, now!" He had a deep voice and knew how to use it. "There's enough fighting without you girls goin' at it."

"She pushed me in." Half drowned or not, Sarah was still a mean little bitch.

"I didn't. She fell. Honest." I looked up at him like he was judge and jury.

He reached down and hauled Sarah up in front of him. "Go on home, Allie. And try to stay out of trouble."

That was better than I maybe deserved, but I felt shamed, and I'd have given anything to be setting on that horse instead of standing there like a mudsill kid. I picked up the doll and handed it over, saw Sarah's nasty little smile that made me hate her all over again. But I wasn't so big a fool as to take her on with him there watching out of those steely eyes.

All I said was: "Next time I won't be around to keep you from drowning. Babies best stick close to their ma." Then I turned and stalked away.

Chapter Three

Thinking about it, I'd bet that some of those kids I played with, fought with, never made it to wherever they was going, or made it as orphans and had to do the best they could. Even though one of 'em, Amelia, who lived down the creek, went West and married ole Brigham Young. I never could figure out why a woman wants to share her man, but, then, there's a lot of things I never figured.

There was always cholera on the trail West, or Injun trouble, or accidents, and the fighting in Kansas got worse every year till the real war started. Not that there was peace like there'd been before, but the wagons stopped, I guess, 'cause most men had gone off with whatever regiment was closest, like Pa.

"I'm goin," he said, and us standing there like dummies, hoping he was fooling. "I'm goin', and that's the end of it. A man's got to fight for what's right."

Mum's face was white, and the lines around her mouth looked like they'd been cut with a knife. "How do you expect we'll get by? Or don't you care?"

"The corn's in. And the garden. And the war can't last forever. You'll make out till I get back."

When Mum got mad, she was fierce. I reckon I got my temper from her. "How come you're so sure you're comin' back? How come you can see the future? You think you're God or something? Well, I ain't God, and I ain't as sure as you, and, if we starve, it'll be on your head, John Sullivan. Goin' off, fightin' for folks you never saw instead of takin' care of your own."

He put his arms around her, but she pushed him away. "Hugs won't help. Go on and go. Just leave the shotgun so we can at least get some meat."

His whole body slumped, and that old man look came back on his face. "If that's the way you want it."

"It's how *you* want it, not me. You and your fine ideas."

He turned to us kids then, telling us to mind our mum and take care of each other. When he got to me, I folded my arms across my middle and looked away. I was his pet, but right then all I felt was that I'd been betrayed.

"No smile for me, Allie?"

I shook my head.

"I'll miss you."

"We'll be too busy starvin' to miss you," I said, and ran out the door pleased with myself but fighting back tears.

Like Mum, I had a feeling he'd not be back. Men got killed in wars. That was what wars was about. Men shooting each other after all the fancy talk and ideas got them no place. Nothing I've seen since has changed my mind about that.

After Pa had gone, we sat around the table looking at each other but nobody saying a word until Lydia started crying. Wasn't a minute before Mary was crying, too.

"You hush that noise!" I told them. "Cryin' don't do any good."

Mum reached out and took them in her arms. "Let them grieve," she said, and she sounded like her own heart was cut out.

20

"What'll we do?" I asked.

"The best we can."

Put that way, it was a challenge, and I never turned away from a dare in my life. As I thought about it, we'd all been working since we was able to walk. Whether Pa was there or not, we had our chores and did them, and, like he'd said, the corn was up, the garden planted, and we still had Sally and the hogs. Besides, there was enough game in those days to feed the whole Union Army, and that river was filled with fish.

I said: "We'll make out fine."

Mum looked down at her belly, and there was fear in her eyes. "If the war don't last forever."

"What's forever?" That was Lydia.

"A long time." She was hiding her fear. Maybe she fooled the young 'uns, but I knew better.

I went to the door and looked out, saw the same things I saw every day, only I saw them different, like in a photograph, as if even then I was trying to take Ponca Bottom away with me. Trees touching a sky so blue it hurt to look. Green corn in dark ground. The different green of punkin leaves and beans, and then, way up, a hawk riding the wind. The world might have changed, but our little place hadn't. It was still beautiful, and it was home, all we had except ourselves. As far as I was concerned, that was enough.

But all we got that summer was hard luck. We had wind, rain, hail that flattened the corn and ruined the garden. We had skunks in the chicken house and a cow that died of water belly. And all the while there was Mum, her legs swelled till she couldn't do more than lay in bed keeping an eye on the girls best she could.

I took over the house chores—the washing, the cooking, what there was to cook. Twelve years old and doing a woman's work, and Mary and Lydia crying much of the time 'cause they didn't understand what had happened, and 'cause they were hungry.

Maybe it was then that I started wondering why anybody'd want kids that had to be cared for, watched over, fed whether there was food to put on the table or not. Maybe it was then I made up my mind I'd never have a child to go hungry, to worry over. Taking care of my own self was hard enough. Hell, life was hard enough. Not that I thought it in those words, but the notion stuck in my head all those years and nothing, not even Virge, ever changed my mind.

Chapter Four

I was out in the garden, hoping to find a squash that hadn't rotted or been chawed on, when Melissa came running. Her hair, that she always kept so neat, was stuck to her cheeks, and her hands were shaking. "The baby's comin'!"

"I'll go for Granny Sykes." I shoved my basket at her, but she pushed it away.

"I'll go. You're better at keepin' her calm. Set the kettle to boil. I'll get back quick as I can find Granny." She went off running, leaving me alone with the kids and Mum who was in bed biting on a rag to keep from screaming.

What I said about not having children turned into a vow that afternoon. Twelve years old and as helpless as a new-hatched chick, and Lydia and Mary holding to my skirts asking what was the matter with Mum.

"She's not feelin' good," I told them. "You want to help, you get the basket and go get us some hazelnuts. Take Frank along."

He looked at me, his bottom lip trembling. "What if you need me?"

"I don't need no little boy. You take care of your sisters. I'll do for Mum."

"How?"

I didn't have an answer, so all I said was: "I'm a girl

same as her. Just stay away till supper."

Supper would be stale cornbread and cold rabbit stew unless the baby came fast. But I remembered how long it took to birth Mary and how I spent most of that day and part of the night scared that Mum was dying and I'd never see her again.

"Allie!" It was a cry for help.

She'd bit her lips till they bled. I wiped her face with a damp rag and started praying, although even then I wasn't sure anybody heard me. *Don't die, Mum. Hold on till Granny and Lissa get here. Where are they? Damn it, what's taking 'em so long?* Not much of a prayer, come to think of it, but I never was good at asking for favors, not even from the Almighty.

"Where's Lissa?" Mum whispered.

"Gone for Granny."

She grabbed my hand. "They'll be too late. Get the water boilin', and get some clean cloths."

I did what she told me, although my hands was shaking like cottonwood leaves. Soon! I hoped not. I knew where babies came from. No farm kid doesn't. But this was different. This was my mum, and there was only us to bring a life into the world. Two of us in the late September heat, flies buzzing through the open door following the stink of sweat and blood.

"Allie!" She sounded like she was strangling. "It's comin!"

When I finally held the little boy in my hands, I was scared I'd drop him, all slippery and squalling like a pig, but I felt something else, too, a happiness, like he was mine, like I'd birthed him myself, and in a way I had.

"Lay him down, and get the knife," Mum said.

For just a second I thought she meant to kill him, and I

stared at her, scared clean through.

She gave what sounded like a laugh. "You got to cut the cord. I'll show you." Her face jerked. "God help us, there's another one comin'."

I stood stockstill. "Another baby?"

"Another mouth to feed," and I heard the tiredness that was more than birth pain.

"Don't quit now."

"I won't. Couldn't if I wanted to."

The second baby was a girl, smaller than her brother but twice as feisty, waving her little arms and yelling till I started laughing, mostly out of relief. I'd done it! Birthed two healthy babies, and hadn't turned squeamish, either, just did like I was told.

"What'll we call 'em?"

Mum sighed. "I used up all the good names. You do it. But wash 'em good first."

She fell asleep without doing more than look at 'em. Maybe she'd seen enough. Maybe she had no more caring in her. No matter. I had enough love to go around. I loved those twins like they was mine, and, as they got older, they thought I was their mum, always holding out their arms for me to pick them up, always calling—"Allie, Allie!"—whenever they saw me.

I named them Cal and Alice, I guess 'cause I liked the sounds, or 'cause once I'd played with a little boy from a wagon train named Cal, and he stuck in my mind. It near broke my heart when us kids got split up, each of us going to a different family, each of us grieving for what was, for the magic of Ponca Bottom, for Mum and Pa, gone too soon to heaven.

Chapter Five

"We're movin' to town." That was Mum, looking like an old woman, her eyes sunk in, her hair gone gray overnight.

"Leave here? We can't! How'll Pa find us?"

She laughed, but it was a laugh with no fun in it. "He'll come if he can. If he wants."

I felt tears, not sad ones but the kind that came with anger, all hot and burning. "Why wouldn't he want? I ain't goin', and you can't make me."

At that Mary and Lydia started crying, too. Frank just stood there looking like he'd been shot between the eyes. "I been doin' the best I can," he mumbled. "It's just . . . well, I'm just a kid."

"I know how hard you worked. It ain't your fault. But another winter here'll do for all of us. At least in town we'll have a chance." Mum wrapped her shawl close around her like she was already feeling the cold. "We can maybe find somebody who wants the farm and have a little money put by for once."

The thing was, the farm was part of me, the part that resisted change, that was the smell of fresh-plowed dirt, the sound of the creek rolling over stones. But I was only a kid, too, and helpless.

Someday, I said to myself, someday I'll be grown and

nobody's going to tear me up by the roots and leave me with no place to call home. Just my luck that I never settled any place long enough to feel I owned it. The Earps, all of 'em, were a restless bunch, never able to stay put, always looking for the big chance. The only real home I ever got was Virge himself. Thinking about that, I have to say he was more than enough.

We were a sorry-looking bunch the day we left, walking 'cause the mule, the wagon, and almost everything else had been sold. It wasn't but a short ways to Omaha, but it felt like we walked a hundred miles, me carrying little Cal, Melissa with Alice, Lydia, and Frank and Mary holding onto Mum who moved so slow it was like we'd never get anywhere.

The sky was filled with birds that day—geese, cranes, ducks—all headed south like us. We could hear the sound of their wings and that strange crying that seemed to come out of heaven, and Mum said they was angels come to watch over us. It wasn't like her to be fanciful or even pay attention to something that happened every year, and the way she said it, kind of like a prayer, gave me something else to worry over. Or maybe it was me being fanciful, because it seemed to me that a part of her was already up there flying with those birds, looking down on us as we set one foot in front of the other, all the time wishing we'd stayed put.

Omaha had been growing the years we'd lived in Ponca Bottom. It was the territorial capital and the place where most of the wagon trains stopped for supplies before heading West. Even during the war it was busy, with boats loading and unloading at the big docks, wagons, horses, mules, people crowding the dusty streets that were lined with what seemed like a hundred saloons.

We stood on the bluffs at the edge of town and gawked like the farmers we were, our mouths open, our eyes popping. Down below was life happening, life that we couldn't even begin to know about, different even than the wagon trains that had come through our place. And all around the hills rising up so gentle, and the grass, the stubble fields, the trees turned the colors of fall, and high up a flock of cranes weaving through the sky like dark lace and calling out.

A funny thing happened to me while I stood there, gawking like a yokel. I saw the land was bigger than all the people on it. It had always been there and always would be, no matter the wagons rolling across, no matter the war, the killing. All we were, any of us, was people, and we wasn't any bigger than the beetles that got the punkins, the grasshoppers that ate whatever they found. And they was more a part of the whole than any of us—Mum, me, the babies, Jim Hickok, the slaves that Pa was fighting for, even Abe Lincoln himself.

I wondered then, but never did figure it out, if Pa hadn't felt the same. If he hadn't gone off to fight for what he thought was a holy place, his land and the land all around that we couldn't see but knew was there. Who knows? I don't. It's only what came over me that day standing there wondering about my future and seeing the river, the hills, the birds that knew where they was headed and who went direct, not like us. They just flew straight on, believing in themselves.

Well, we found rooms in a boarding house owned by a Mrs. Cain. Her husband was off to the war, too, and she had to find a way to support herself. She asked if Melissa and me wanted to work. If we did, we could have our room for free. We said yes and went to scrubbing and washing just like at home, while Mum stayed upstairs and took care

of the girls and the twins. A livery stable that had a room for
him in the hayloft hired Frank, and we didn't see much of
him except when he came for his supper.

For a while it looked like we'd make it. But one day,
when I was in the kitchen peeling potatoes, Mrs. Cain came
in. "Allie," she said, "what will you do when your Mum's
gone?"

I didn't understand. "She ain't goin' anywhere."

"She's dyin', Allie."

At that the knife I was using slipped, and I cut the tip of
my finger and stood there, watching the blood drip all over
the spuds. It was like seeing my own life run out of me slow.

"A lot you know," I said after a while. "She's my mum,
and I'd know if she was dyin'."

She put a hand on my shoulder. "Allie. . . ."

"She ain't! When Pa gets home, she'll get better. You
wait and see."

"It feels like this war won't ever end," she said.

I thought the same, but wouldn't admit it. Not to her.
"It has to stop sometime, don't it?"

She gave a sigh, and I remembered that her husband had
sent her a letter from a place called Shiloh, and she kept
that letter under her blouse against her heart like it was a
piece of him, and she wasn't letting go.

"I don't know, child," she said. "I really don't know.
Maybe, when they're all dead and there's nobody left to
fight, it'll stop." Then she went out and stood in the yard
crying, but not wanting me to see. It was like Melissa had
said a long time before. Men go to war, and the women stay
home and worry and weep.

I wrapped a piece of rag around my finger and went back
to peeling potatoes. The one thing I knew was that crying
didn't help. All the time wasted on tears was better spent

doing something about the problem. But what I was supposed to do about Mum, I didn't know.

The day of her funeral was one of those still, cold days that came before a hard storm. The wind smelled like snow, and the ground was froze so hard they had a time of it digging the hole deep enough to fit the coffin. We spent most of our savings on that plain wood box, but none of us wanted our mum laid to rest without something that said we cared.

Hardly anybody came to the burying—Mrs. Cain, a few gray-faced men I didn't know, a preacher somebody had found and drug in, and who I hated at first glance, and the Injun woman we called Mary 'cause we never could get the hang of her Injun name. She was a good sort, had been a friend to us a long time, and was always laughing, but that morning her face was set like a stone, even when she held out her arms for little Cal.

"I take," she said. "I keep him safe for you."

"No!" I wasn't about to send him off with the Injuns, no matter how much I liked her.

"Better me." Her black eyes took in the others with distrust.

And then I understood. Somebody was going to take the twins away, take my little brother and sister who thought I was their mum, and I'd never see them, never hear them laugh again.

I held Cal tighter. "My pa's comin'. It'll be all right then."

Her eyes told me I was a fool living in a fool's dream, but she didn't answer, just shook her head and pulled her greasy blanket tight. "Your mother good to me. Good lady. Maybe she happy now. Maybe you be happy one day." Then she walked away.

Maybe Mum was happy, I thought. Maybe she was up there flying with those birds and watching over us. But I wasn't about to bet on it. I never was one for make-believe. Fairy tales, like dolls in fancy clothes, wasn't for the likes of me, no matter how much I wished otherwise.

The funeral was over, and the snow was coming down steady. I could hear it beating against the window, hear the wind moaning like it was lost. We was sitting around the big dinner table back at Mrs. Cain's—her, the preacher, the two men I'd seen at the burying, and us kids holding hands like we knew what was coming.

"Understand. I have a business to run." That was Mrs. Cain looking miserable. "I can use Allie and Melissa, but I got no time to spare taking care of a family. Better this way for you all."

We was orphans now, they'd told us. And orphans went where they was sent, did what they was told, and had no say about it. In those days there was plenty of folks who'd take an orphan and use that child as free labor—on the farm, in the house, just like those slaves my pa was fighting for. It was like kids was just things to be handed around, used, and either got broken or survived.

The preacher cleared his throat and started talking in that way I always thought was slimy—as if he was better than us and had a connection with God. "The Orchards are good people," he began, and cleared his throat again. "But God hasn't seen fit to give them children of their own. Cal and Alice will be taken care of. I can promise you that. Believe me when I say I am with you in your sorrow, but the Lord giveth, and He taketh away, and He has seen fit to call your mother to eternal life."

It was all pompous bullshit, and I wanted no part of him

or his do-good plan. "Mum took sick. 'Twasn't God's doin'."

He pulled himself up and looked at me like I was a toad that had hopped up on the table. "Be quiet!" Spit flew out of his mouth and landed on the nice, shiny wood that I'd polished myself. "Little girls do not speak back to their elders."

"I'm almost grown." I was more than ready to take him on, defend my family with all I had.

Mrs. Cain reached across the table toward me. "Hush, Allie. Mind your manners. He . . . we are only trying to help."

I shook her off. "Can't you see? We got to stay together. What'll Pa do when he comes back and we're all split up? How's he going to find us?"

The preacher interrupted. "It's up to us to do what's best for you. Someday you'll think back and be grateful."

I wanted to kick him. I wanted to spit back right in his face, then grab hold of the twins and run till I couldn't run no more, maybe back to Ponca Mary's village. It was only the storm that kept me there, the snow and the wind hollering. Only a fool would take babies out in that. I was helpless, but nobody ever called me dumb.

I pushed back from the table and stood as tall as I could, which wasn't much. To Mrs. Cain I said: "Thank you for keepin' me and Lissa on. We're grateful for that and for what you done. But . . . ."—I looked that preacher straight in the eye—"but I'm damned if I'll thank you for handin' my family to strangers."

As I ran out of the room, I heard the preacher's pronouncement. "That one will come to a bad end. Mark my words."

A fat lot he knew! And I'm not at my end yet!

Chapter Six

When the war was over, the men started coming home.
Yankees and Confederates, they came on foot, on horseback, by boat, every one ragged, all of 'em looking defeated
no matter what side they had fought on. Four years had
turned them into men who'd seen too much, done things
they didn't talk about, made every one a stranger in his own
home.

Like Mr. Cain who got back with a stump and a peg leg
that had his wife crying harder than ever and fussing over
him like a hen with one chick. It was a good thing the
boarding house business was booming, 'cause he didn't
seem like he'd ever work at much again.

For some reason, he took a liking to me, and sometimes,
after I'd washed up the supper dishes, we'd sit on the back
porch and talk, or maybe not say much at all, just watch
night coming on, admiring the big moths that fluttered
around, attracted to the light of the lamp burning in the
kitchen. I thought maybe he'd run across Pa during the
fighting, but he said not. Said even if he had, there was no
way of knowing where Pa was now or if he'd been taken
prisoner.

"Don't set your heart on him coming, Allie," he said one
night. "More of us died in Southern prisons than in the

fighting." His mouth twisted. "It'd been better if I'd died, too. What I am now is pretty sorry."

That set my back up. "You wouldn't talk like that if you knew how Missus Cain missed you. She carried your letters on her, and read them all the time, and cried her heart out. Maybe, instead of sittin' here feelin' sorry for yourself, you should go tell her you love her."

"Easy for you to say."

"Lovin' a person ain't hard."

He gave what passed for a laugh. "You're young yet, Allie."

"I ain't so young I don't know how things are."

The gate at the end of the yard clicked open, and Melissa and Tom came through. They'd been walking out for months, and we was all watching the courtship with interest. Every morning at breakfast, Mr. Cain would say: "Did he pop the question yet, Lissa?" And she'd blush and stammer and finally say he hadn't, much to Mrs. Cain's relief. She didn't want to lose the help, but wasn't about to stand in Melissa's way.

That night it was different. Melissa and Tom came to where we was sitting and stood there with grins on their faces.

"I reckon you have something to tell us." Mr. Cain was grinning back at them.

Tom cleared his throat, and for one awful second I was reminded of that preacher. But when he spoke, he was his own self and pleased with it. "I asked Lissa if she could stand to be married to me."

"And I said yes!" Her eyes was shining even in the dark.

"When's the weddin'?" I asked.

"Soon as we can. And . . . and we were wonderin', Mister Cain, if you'd give me away."

He looked down at his peg leg, then back at her. "If you don't mind helpin' an old cripple walk up the aisle, I'd be proud to."

"Maybe Pa will be back by then," I put in.

Nobody answered, just looked at me like they was sorry for me, holding on to what wasn't there.

"If he's back," Melissa said, "they can both do it. One on each side of me."

Later, though, when we were in bed, she propped herself up on one elbow and spoke her mind. "It's time you stopped lookin' for Pa every time you see a man on the street. It's time you got it in your head that we'll never all be together again. Pa ain't comin' home. Mum knew it, and it killed her, don't say it didn't. Maybe he got killed, or maybe he'd had enough. Of the farm or of us. Mum always said he was too restless for his own good, always lookin' for a place nobody else had found yet. We're on our own, Allie, and we got to do the best we can. Now be happy for me, and stop hopin'."

All I could say was: "But Pa loved us."

"Sure he did. But sometimes love's not enough. Sometimes it wears out, God help me."

She sounded like Mr. Cain. Like she'd left a piece of herself behind at the farm. But unlike him, she didn't miss it, not one bit. Her eyes were on the future and her life with Tom.

"When we're married, you can come live with us," she said.

"And scrub your floors?"

That hurt her. She pulled away, lips trembling. "You know better than that. We've got to stick together. We're all that's left."

"And you've got Tom."

She punched her pillow like she wished it was me. "How come you're so prickly? How come you always got a smart answer? Why can't you just wish me well and be happy?"

Now the funny thing was that I never took the time to figure if I was happy or not. That was for others. I just went on doing what had to be done, and, although I grieved over my family, I didn't know I was unhappy till she said it.

I reached out for her hand. It was as chapped and callused from hard work as my own. "I get along fine."

"Sure. But it's no fun. Just wait, though. You'll find somebody and get married, too, someday."

"Maybe."

"Oh, you will. Though he'll have to be deaf to put up with your mouth. But you wait and see."

"I see enough as it is, and most of it's a misery."

"There you go again!" She gave the pillow another punch, then chuckled, that sound that made me think of the creek back home. "Let's forget all this. It's gettin' us no place. Let's plan what to wear at my weddin'."

I only had one dress, so planning wasn't a problem, but I went along with her. "That'll make you happy?" I asked.

"Yes," she said, "it sure will."

Right around the time of the wedding, the Cains started fighting. I think the missus had got fed up with him sitting out there, never lifting a hand to help. Peg leg or not, he was strong and healthy enough once he got some decent grub in him.

Whatever the reason, she henpecked that man till it seemed we'd never have any peace in the house, and I felt sorrier for him than ever 'cause all he was after was peace.

The Cains was Catholics, and every couple of weeks a priest would come out, and do a service in the old schoolhouse. I never went, never had no need of praying, though Mrs. Cain kept after me.

"It's not right, Allie," she'd say. "You growin' up without religion. I can't figure what your mum was thinkin' because it's a heathen you are, and that's a fact."

I mostly ignored her, but I was curious about what went on the afternoons before the Sunday service, when the Cains and the other Catholics in the neighborhood lined up and went inside, one by one, most of 'em looking like they was going to a hanging.

"We're confessing our sins," Mrs. Cain explained to me. "We're wiping our souls clean for Jesus."

Well, I couldn't see the right of that. Telling your sins couldn't take 'em away, not as far as I was concerned. What's done is done, but maybe the Catholics had some secret I should know about just in case. So the next time the priest came, I went to the school and pulled a piece of chinking out of the log wall. Then I settled down to watch.

Inside, there was a piece of blanket hanging from a line, and the priest sat on one side, the folks telling their sins on the other. And let me tell you, I heard things that day that like to set my ears on fire! Truth be told, I'd rather not have known what the neighbors or our boarders was up to. I never could look some of 'em in the face again for fear they'd know what I'd heard.

By the time Mrs. Cain came in with a raggedy shawl on her head, I was wishing I was some place else, but I was powerful nosey about what she was going to say. She started with a list of things I thought were plain foolish, and then she got to the fighting between her and her husband, making it sound like she was the one put upon.

"And who is it starts this fighting?" the priest asked, his voice loud and carrying what sounded to me like a threat.

"My husband." She actually sounded like she was crying. "It's always him that starts it."

Now that didn't sit right with me, and, as far as I ever heard, lying's as big a sin as any other. I just couldn't let her get away with telling a lie, so I shouted out as loud as I could: "And you're a liar! Every time it's been you started it! And poor Mister Cain sitting there with his one leg."

Well, the two of 'em popped out of their chairs like they'd been shot and ran for the door. Me, I just ran, fast as I could, figuring I was going to get a whipping or get sacked for sure.

I climbed the pasture fence, and the pony the Cains kept for their kids, and that I rode, too, was standing there, looking like he wanted company, so I crawled up on him and we took off. I rode around a long time, wondering if I dared go back to the house, but I didn't have no place else to go, and it was getting too dark to see, so I figured I'd go take my medicine.

When I walked in the kitchen, Mrs. Cain was at the stove same as always. She gave me a look and said: "There you are. I was wondering where you'd got to. Get a pan and shell those peas for me, then set a place for Father. He's stayin' for supper." That was all. I sat there, shelling peas and waiting for what I knew was coming, but she never said another word.

The priest was a fat old man with white eyebrows that hung down in his eyes like the pony's forelock. He never said nothing, neither, and I ate my supper, squirming in my chair.

When we finished, the old man folded his hands. "We'll say our beads now."

I had no idea what he meant, and it must've showed on

my face, because he looked square at me and said: "Child, where are your beads?"

I thought he was talking about a necklace. "I never had one," I said, wishing I was some place else.

"Then I'll bring you a rosary next time I come."

"I . . . ," was all I got out before Mrs. Cain interrupted.

"Allie's not Catholic, Father."

"Ah." He frowned, like not being Catholic was a worse sin than the lies and fornication I'd heard about all afternoon. "What are you then?"

I thought about that a minute, not sure what he was asking. Then Mrs. Cain's words came back to me. "I'm a heathen!" I shouted out. "That's what I am."

Those white eyebrows shot up like a pair of bird wings. "And who told you that?"

"Missus Cain!"

Everybody laughed but him and me. He turned serious. "Tell me, do you believe in God, child?"

I thought some more. Thought about what happened to Pa and Mum, about happiness taken away before any of us knew we'd had it. And, for no reason, I thought about those cranes flying over our heads, making their journey year after year, and Mum watching them, her eyes lit up like stars.

"I reckon I do sometimes."

He reached over and patted my hand. "Then that's enough. But I'll pray that you come to believe in Him all the time."

He wasn't like that preacher they'd got to bury Mum. Actually he was kindly, so I didn't say anything, for once. The funny thing was that nobody, not even Mrs. Cain, ever mentioned that day again. And the fighting between her and her husband kept right on going.

★ ★ ★ ★ ★

Six months later, I got the sack, probably because after that day Mrs. Cain never could quite trust me. But her excuse was the fact that one of the boarders, a Mr. Porter, got smart with me when I was serving the soup. Got smart and patted me where he shouldn't, and got hot soup in his lap and a telling off from me.

Mrs. Cain was mad. Can't say I blame her, but I couldn't blame myself, neither. "I'll be lucky if he doesn't make me pay for his suit," she said. We were in the kitchen, the door to the dining room tight shut. "What on earth got into you?"

"Maybe next time he'll think before he goes feelin' a girl's bottom," I said. "Maybe he'll keep his hands and his pecker to himself."

That shocked her. She backed up a step and looked at me like I was poison—or that heathen child she'd never been able to change. "You'll have to go. Some of the things that come out of your mouth . . . well, I can't put up with them."

Sure, I thought, *like me telling that priest the truth.* But all I said was: "Tonight?"

"Tomorrow's soon enough. I'll have your pay ready in the morning. Though, if he wants money for his suit, you won't get much. In the meantime, stay out of his sight." She sighed. "I hope you learn something from this, Allie."

What I'd learned was that liars protect themselves from themselves, and that men were out for what they could get. As far as I was concerned, Porter got what he deserved. I went out on the porch where Mr. Cain was whittling on a stick of wood.

"You get sacked?" he asked.

"Yeah."

"What'll you do?"

40

"Get by. I ain't helpless."

He laughed. "Reckon old Porter found that out."

"He's a dirty old man."

"Most of us are, one time or another."

I stared at him, wondering just what he meant. "Not you."

He worked on his whittling a minute. "Not any more, anyhow. A wood leg puts an end to that kind of thing. Come back and see me once in a while if you think of it. I'll miss sitting out here with you."

"Best talk to your wife," I told him. "And try not to fight, even if she is the one that starts it. Fightin' just tears folks apart, and what's the good of it?"

He shook his head. "The world does that. I'm not the man she married, and she's not how I remember her. And I reckon there's lots like us around."

I wondered how it would've been if Pa'd come back with a peg leg and no way to keep on farming. Still, I reckoned Mum would've done the best she could, and would've forgiven him for going off like he did.

"Folks change," I said after a bit. "But that don't change the fact you're married."

"You're right there." He went back to whittling. "Don't pay me no mind, Allie. I can live with the fighting. It's nothing to where I was, what I saw and can't forget. But that's not your problem. You just take care of yourself, hear?"

"Guess I'll have to, seein's there's nobody to do it for me."

Something about the way he sat there, his head hanging, his shoulders slumped, got to me. I hoped that, if Pa was still alive, he wasn't broken like this man was, hoped that he'd kept the pride that I remembered so well, and the way he could laugh at most anything, even troubles.

I said: "I thank you and your missus for takin' me in. I'll miss sittin' out here with you, too." Then I went in and started packing.

Chapter Seven

I put my foot down about living with Melissa and Tom being as they was just married and didn't really want to have company.

"Independent as a hog on ice. That's you," Virge used to tell me when I dug in my heels over something.

Well, I came by it natural, and I wasn't any different at sixteen and on my own in Omaha. There was always work for anybody who'd do it. I took care of babies, scrubbed floors, waited tables, sold dry goods, and did the washing for the biggest whorehouse in town. The girls, most of 'em no older than me, made me a pet, said I was no bigger than the cooties some of the customers left behind.

Mollie, the madam, gave me a bed to sleep on behind the kitchen stove. "You won't be bothered back here," she said with a grin. "Unless you want to be."

"I don't want a bunch of brats."

She shrugged. "If you change your mind, there's ways out of that."

"And some of 'em don't work."

Another shrug. "Of course. We all know that. But you're a smart girl. Like me. Keep yourself to yourself and save your money. It and you is safer that way."

She was smart, all right. She hoarded the money her girls

made on their backs. Kept it in a big safe she'd got from somewhere, and planned for the day she'd quit the business and set up as a rich widow some place where nobody knew her. I don't know if that ever happened, but I hope so. For all she ran a house, she was a good woman, kinder than a lot of the madams I met in my life, although later, when I met Bessie Earp, I had to say that she was as nice a woman as I ever met.

I learned things in that house that served me well, but at the top of the list was Mollie's advice. I wasn't about to be pawed over by any man and then left. I wasn't going to be a body without a brain in it, a doll with a smile painted on to hide the misery. I might have to go hungry, I might not have a place to sleep, but I was damned if I'd ever sell myself to whoever came along looking for a poke.

Mollie was a big believer in cleanliness. Her house was closed Wednesday afternoons, and the girls, and me, took our baths. Then I changed the sheets and started in washing.

Mollie had a Negro woman, Antonia, in the kitchen, and what she couldn't do with a chicken or a catfish ain't worth telling. I never afterwards fried a trout or a catfish that I didn't hear that soft voice saying: "Cracker crumbs do better than cornmeal, honey. I don't know why, they just does. And, you want to fry a chicken, get you some buttermilk, and use lots of it." Whatever I learned about cooking came from hanging around Antonia, keeping my eyes and ears open. If I ever get asked where I went to school, I'd have to say—"Mollie's whorehouse."—and wouldn't that get me a look?

I'd have to say that's where I got my first taste of whiskey, too. It was my time of month, and I was hobbling around, bent over, holding my stomach when Antonia took pity on me. She always had a bottle that she'd pinched off Mollie and hidden somewhere, and that day she called me into the kitchen.

"Here," she said. "This'll help."

I took the glass and drank that whiskey down like it was water, then stood there gasping for breath like a landed fish.

"Lordy, honey, you supposed to drink it slow."

Whether or not I could breathe, I could feel that stuff warming my belly, and I held out the glass for more.

She frowned at me. "I don't know as you oughta."

"Oh, come on," I said. "I've watched you takin' drinks out of that bottle more than once."

"I'm older'n you."

"Yeah, but you won't always be."

She let out a chuckle. "Guess that's so. And there's times a person's only comfort's a good bottle. But you go easy now."

I got a little light-headed, but not so much anybody noticed.

Antonia wasn't happy. "You got a hollow leg, honey. You watch it don't take you over and you blame me for teachin' you."

Well, it never did, but I never turned down a drink of whiskey, either. Still don't if I get offered one. There's been times since I lost Virge that only a stiff drink could get me over my grieving, and I don't see it's anybody's business if that's so.

I had another friend, Fannie, one of the girls. Mollie had found her wandering the streets across the river in Council Bluffs. She was one of those wagon train orphans whose folks had died off and who got left to make it or not.

One day I was outside, struggling to get the sheets hung out. The line was too high, and I'd taken to using a little three-legged stool so I could reach. It was hard work, climbing up with a wet sheet, pinning it tight, then climbing back down for the next. Almost as hard as stirring the wash in the big kettles, then wringing everything out by hand. At night my arms ached so bad it was a pure pleasure to be able to lie down on my cot and stretch out as far as I could. Sometimes, on nights like those, I'd sneak into the kitchen and take a nip out of Antonia's bottle. If she knew, she never said.

But hanging clothes was how I got to know Fannie. She came out of the bathhouse and stood watching me, then walked over to where I was. She grabbed a sheet out of my hands and had it up and drying before I got my mouth open.

"I'm taller than you," she said. "Why don't I help a while?"

"It ain't your job."

"No. But I've got an hour, and I'm tired being inside all the time. I like it outside better."

She had a mess of red hair, and freckles, and a smile that was real, not put on for show.

"Why you workin' here, then?" I asked. "You like doin' what you do?"

She made a face. "It beats going hungry. It beats not havin' a place to sleep, and Mollie treats us good."

"But you could work anywhere. Look at me."

"Mollie found me first. I was on the street and starving, and she brought me here. So I'm grateful. And I've got used to it. It's not so bad after the first couple times. You'd be surprised."

I would, and that's a fact. What goes on between a man and a woman's different when love comes into it. I knew that even as a kid, don't ask how. But what Virge and I had was precious, and I'll wager no whore ever said that about a customer no matter who he was, how nice he was.

It was Fannie who showed me how to keep from having babies. A sponge soaked in vinegar or a lump of cocoa butter'd do it, she said. And if they didn't work, there was always a dose of pennyroyal or a knitting needle. But there wasn't no sure way, and Fannie found that out. She got caught, and, instead of telling Mollie, she tried to get rid of it herself.

I was hanging up towels when Pegeen, one of the girls, ran out of the bathhouse like the devil was nipping her heels. "Where's Mollie? Fannie's bleedin' all over the place."

I dropped the towel I was holding, never mind I'd have to wash it over. "What happened?"

"Knitting needle." Her face told me the rest.

"How come she didn't tell Mollie? Why'd she try it herself?"

"She didn't want to lose her job. Figured she could take care of it and nobody'd find out." Pegeen wiped her nose on her sleeve.

"Run, get Mollie," I said. "I'll go see what I can do for Fan."

If I was the kind that fainted at the sight of blood, I'd have fainted dead away in that bathhouse. I never knew we had that much blood in us till I saw Fannie lying there. Her face was dead white, and that red hair of hers looked like it was on fire. For a minute I thought she was already gone, but she opened her eyes and looked at me.

"I guess I'm done for." It was the littlest whisper.

"Mollie's comin'. She'll know what to do. Just lay still." I folded a towel and put it under her head, and then put another between her legs. It turned red in a minute.

She started crying. "Now I'll go to hell."

"You won't, either. The devil don't want you." It was a sorry excuse for a joke, but better that than bawling myself.

"It was wrong, what I did. Seems like everything I've done was wrong."

I took hold of her hand. It was cold as ice, and for once I thought about what to say before I opened my mouth. "Doin' what you have to, what you think you have to when you got no choice ain't wrong. You got to give God credit for a little sense instead of whippin' yourself."

She tried to smile, but it turned into pain. "You sound like a priest."

"And me a heathen," I said. "But I'm just Allie, and I know what's what."

Mollie came in then and knelt down on the floor. After one look she said: "Go get old Doc Turner, and get him quick."

But we never did stop the bleeding. Even the doctor said there wasn't much he could do except carry her inside and make her comfortable. At the end, Fannie never knew she was dying, and I was glad about that. She'd been a good friend.

We all pitched in and gave her a decent burial, and that night I packed my one good dress, the cameo brooch that had been Mum's, my night shift, and a pair of stockings I'd darned so much they looked more like a quilt. Then I went to find Mollie.

She was sitting behind her big desk not doing much except stare out the window.

"I'm leavin'," I said.

"Because of Fannie?"

I nodded.

"I'm sorry. For her and for you havin' to see that."

"Me, too. She didn't have to go that way."

Mollie's mouth made a straight line. "She was a damn' fool. If I'd known, it wouldn't have happened. There's better ways. Even havin' the kid's better than dyin'. You sure you don't want to take her place?"

I gave a snort. "I ain't no damn' fool."

"I didn't think so, but thought I'd ask." She got up and went to the safe, spun the dial, and pulled out a sack. Then she counted out what looked to me to be a lot of money and handed it to me. "I'll miss you. Me and the girls. What'll you do now?"

I reckoned I could go anywhere with that money, one best dress, and a good pair of boots. But that country along the Missouri, the wide sky, the rolling prairie still held me. That and the fact that Melissa was living in Council Bluffs, and I still had hopes that maybe Pa would come back and find us.

"I reckon I'll stick around a while and see."

That was the smartest decision I ever made. If I'd up and left, I'd never have met Virge, never had all those years I miss so much.

Chapter Eight

"I come to scrub your floors."

Melissa turned away from the pot full of greasy water and dirty dishes, saw me, and started crying. She'd had a hard time of it. Tom was laid up after being run over by a freight wagon—another damned fool the way I saw it—and, with no money coming in, she'd opened her own boarding house. That was a smart move, seeing as how Council Bluffs was growing, but she had more work than she could handle. She was worn out, all skin and bones, her hair hanging every which way and looking like she hadn't washed it in a month.

I held out my arms, and she ran into them like a kid looking for comfort from its ma, and I thought how funny it was, me taking care of her and about to tell her what to do.

"Go sit in that chair. Is there any coffee left?"

She gave what I took for a nod, hard to tell with her head on my shoulder.

"Then sit. We'll have a cup. The dishes ain't goin' no-where."

She plopped down and watched me without saying a word. I had to wash two cups and find a rag to dry them, and, by the time the coffee was hot, she'd wiped her face and on it was a hint of her old smile.

"That's better," I said.

She took a sip. "No more whorehouse laundry?"

"Don't get snippy. Not when I come to help, like I said. I come to do whatever you need, and it looks like I'm just in time. Now . . ."—I held out my hand—"don't start bawlin' again. Tears don't help."

She plunked her elbows on the table and rested her chin in her hands. "It's been so hard with Tom in bed needing me for everything, and men tracking in mud and getting mad when their supper's late. I didn't think it'd be so hard, even though I worked for Missus Cain and should've known."

"Mum had it worse than you, me, or Missus Cain," I reminded her.

"I guess growin' up I never noticed. There was always a bunch of us to help out. Here there's just me."

I sipped my own coffee, black and strong. "You got any sweetening?"

"In the cupboard. You sound just like one of my boarders. He puts molasses on everything."

"How many boarders are there?" The house wasn't big, and I was wondering where I'd sleep.

"Four right now. They double up. And none of them stay very long. There's a couple of freighters, and some railroad men. They don't make trouble and they pay without complaining. That's what keeps us going."

The railroad. I only hoped it didn't get built all the way West till I had my chance to travel in a wagon with good horses pulling it. Going somewhere fast was fine for those who didn't want to see anything. For me, I couldn't ever see enough of the world. For me, every bit of land, every turn on the trail was a gift, down to the littlest stone.

"You're dreamin' again, Allie," she said.

"There ain't nothin' wrong with dreamin'," I told her. "It's what keeps most folks goin', or would if they had sense." But I got up, grabbed an apron off a hook, and started on the dishes.

She made a move to help me, but I waved her off. "Put your feet up and set. Like I told you, I'm here to do what's needed. And tomorrow we're washing your hair. You look a fright."

She looked like I'd slapped her, but she came right back at me. "You're no beauty, either."

"I never said I was. But I keep myself decent. And your boarders won't thank you if they get cooties from sleepin' in your beds. See what that does for your business."

She shivered. "I never thought about that."

"Then it's time to start. And speakin' of bugs, where can I sleep?"

Her mouth dropped open. "Lord, Allie, there's no place. I've got beds squeezed in every corner. What'll we do?"

"I don't take no room. A closet'll do for me."

In the end, we found space behind the stove. Closet don't describe it. But there was room enough for me to get dressed, and it was always warm in winter. In summer, well, that was different, but I got used to it.

Now that I'm thinking back, I see I've spent years getting dressed behind one kitchen stove or another. But I got no complaints. And after two years at Melissa's, the best and happiest part of my life began. It started like this.

Chapter Nine

First thing I noticed about the man standing in the door was how his eyes twinkled. Like he had some private joke he wasn't telling, or maybe he was laughing at me. I was setting the big table for supper. Had just put out the bread and a plate of the pickles I'd made from the garden. They looked so good, I sneaked one, and then another, and the big stranger saw me.

"Don't stand there, laughin'," I said to him. "I grew 'em, I made 'em, I reckon I can eat 'em. Now what can I do for you?"

He gave a little bow just like a gentleman, but he was still grinning at me like he'd caught me with my hand in the cookie jar. "Virgil Earp. I'm staying here. Mostly because the word's out you make the best pickles east of the river."

He was so tall I had to tilt my head back near to my shoulders to see him right, but at that first look everything around me seemed to stand still, like the world had quit breathing just for a minute. I heard Melissa banging pots in the kitchen, the clock on the dresser ticking away, the thump of my heart in time with a voice in my head that kept saying my name, Allie, Allie, like it was trying to tell me something.

When everything got back to normal, he was still there,

eyes twinkling, white teeth showing under that reddish blond mustache, and I knew I was hooked, me, who'd said often enough I didn't want nothing to do with a man.

"Supper's not for ten minutes," I got out, hoping he hadn't noticed my confusion.

"Can I have a pickle while I'm waiting?"

It beats me how the most ordinary conversation can cover up what's not being talked about. How we could stand there and say words, but all the time be leaning toward each other like a pair of magnets. That's how it was with us, and neither wanting to admit it, maybe scared to. I know I was. And later Virge told me he felt just the same, like he'd been pole-axed and wasn't sure what had happened.

All I said then was—"Sure. There's plenty more."—and scooted out to the kitchen before I made a fool out of myself.

"Who's this man, Earp?" I asked Melissa.

She was frying spuds in a big iron pan. "He's drivin' the stage between here and Des Moines. Why?"

"Just askin'."

She glanced at me over her shoulder. "Your face is all red. You comin' down with something?"

I was, for sure, had already caught it, but not the sickness she had in mind. "It's hot in here."

"Well, open the door. And hand me that bowl. Then go ring the dinner bell."

I can still see him at that table, bigger than all the rest of them and better mannered, too. Ma Earp mightn't have been able to read or write, but she saw to it that all her kids knew how to eat right and chew with their mouths shut. Nothing bothers me more than seeing somebody's half-chewed dinner dribbling down their chin.

Virge watched me serving, still all twinkly-eyed, like he was waiting for me to say or do something, or like he was taking the whole of me into his head and wouldn't forget. I'm old, but in my heart I'm that young girl, moving around my sister's table, trying not to spill or make a fool of myself just because a stranger had knocked me endways.

That young writer fella never got any of that part of me—about how it is when a woman finds the one man made for her. He wasn't interested in me, anyhow. All he thought about was Tombstone and Wyatt, and the street fight, and the money he'd make lying about what the Earps had really done, making them out to be no better than scum.

Well, the Earps did a lot of things that folks today won't understand, like gambling and such, but they was all God-fearing men who never backed away from doing right. Their old lady saw to that. Tough as mule meat she was, with a heart that was pure gold.

I'm sitting here in my room getting mad all over again at that fella. At how he got me going, and then turned every damned thing I said around, put words in my mouth so it seems like I betrayed the Earps and myself, too.

Better calm down, Allie, I say. Get a hold of yourself. Listen for the voices you can't ever forget and to hell with the man who can't hold a candle to the men you knew. A man who ain't worth spitting on.

There's Virge saying: "You haven't told me your name."

And me sounding like a bell with a crack in it. "Allie. Allie Sullivan."

"It suits you. At least, when you're not eatin' a sour pickle."

Did it? I guess so. I never could stand the name Alvira, never used it if I could help it. Sounds like an old spinster with spectacles and prissy ways to me. I always wondered what got into Mum, calling me that.

But I reckon we never really understand another person. Even with Virge, there was places in him I couldn't reach, things he kept to himself. The Earp men was all like that. Quiet about a lot of things. There was that Ellen Rysdam who Virge had got in trouble back when he lived in Iowa. We'd been together a long time before I found out about her, and that was by chance when Virge found out about the daughter he never knew he had.

"Why didn't you tell me?" I wanted to know. "All this time, you never said nothin'."

He tugged on his mustache. "I never knew myself. I went off to war, and, when I got back, she was gone without leaving me a note or sayin' anything, and I heard she was dead. Anyhow, what's the use of going over old mistakes? You might take it in your head to leave me."

The look in his eyes made me warm all over. "I won't ever leave you. I'm stuck to you like a tick to a dog's belly."

"You say the damnedest things!" Virge was laughing, but he understood. He reached down, put his hands around my waist, picked me up, and kissed me till my head reeled.

See, from that first night at Melissa's, there was that between us, that tug toward each other, and there wasn't no getting away from it or trying to pretend it wasn't there. It's still there, although Virge has been gone over thirty years. Seems like I can still hear him calling me.

Come for a walk with me, Miss Allie Sullivan. The dishes can wait, but I can't.

I couldn't wait, either, but he wasn't going to order me around like he owned me. I tossed him a towel. "It'll go faster if you help."

He caught the towel with one hand, and I thought he

was going to make a smart answer, but Melissa had to have her say. "Boarders ain't supposed to help in the kitchen. Excuse my sister's manners, Mister Earp. You two go on. I can finish up."

"Manners got nothin' to do with it," I muttered, and kept on scrubbing like I hadn't heard her.

And Virge, well, he just laughed that big, booming laugh and dried those dishes so fast I couldn't keep up. When we was finished, he tossed the towel back at me, untied my apron quick as a wink, and took hold of my arm.

I said: "I need my bonnet."

"Leave it. It's a shame to hide such pretty hair."

Being as much a fool over a man's flattery as any girl, I went with him out the door.

Chapter Ten

Early evening along the river, the sun almost down, the bluffs on the other side fading to a color I never saw any other place, a color that brings to mind how sweet grass smells in the rain, and how stubble fields in October tell you summer's gone. It's the smell and feel of being young with a yearning for what's to come and a sadness for what's already past.

I didn't have words for all this then and don't now, but there's times when I can remember back so plain, see things so clear I'd like to bust open like one of them milkweed pods that's filled up with seeds. Blow on 'em and they float away on the air all silvery in the sun. That's how I'd like my words to be, but they ain't, and I'm too old to learn better.

That evening I just walked along, taking everything in and feeling like I'd come home. Funny, I never figured I'd fall for a man as big as Virge. We sure always looked mismatched, me trotting alongside him like the runt of the litter. But it never really mattered to us. Not at all.

I told him about my family, how I still went looking for Pa, and how I'd probably never see most of them again. Cal and Alice had disappeared, and Frank had caught a fever he couldn't seem to shake and died the year after I went to Melissa's. Mary and Lydia had gone with their new families, although sometimes Melissa had letters from wherever they'd got to. But I told Virge how lonely it felt sometimes, knowing there wasn't nobody but me, and that life went on no matter what.

He listened without saying a word, just listened, his head bent down toward me to catch every word. He always was a good listener, taking everything in before passing judgment. It's what made him and his brothers good lawmen later. They never went off half-cocked like so many others—the outlaws, the crazies, the riff-raff that made up most of Tombstone and near every place else they ever went.

"Reckon I came along at just the right time," he said when I'd got quiet.

"For what?" I knew he was coming on to me but figured to make him work a little.

"To save you. Bein' lonely and all."

"I don't need savin'."

He smiled. "From yourself, I mean."

That got to me. "I'm fine the way I am."

"Yeah," he said. "Prickly as a porcupine, sour as a pickle. One of these days you'll stick yourself. Then what?"

"Then I'll fix it."

He sure had a strange way of courting. Maybe I'd misread him, after all. A girl don't take kindly to being called a porcupine. On the other hand, I hadn't been exactly full of sweet talk myself. It'd serve me right if he left and I never saw him again. Now I never was one of those simpering misses batting my eyes and giggling like a five-year-old, but I figured I'd better start and quick.

I put my hand on his arm just like any young miss, and started talking. "What's it like drivin' a stage? What's it like out there? I never been anywhere but here and across the river."

He thought a minute, or maybe my hand on his arm had stolen his voice. "Pretty dull," he said. "Same road, same places unless we get caught by a tornado or a blizzard. It's not what I want to do the rest of my life."

"What do you want?"

He bent down, picked a piece of grass, and chewed the end. "Maybe get me a farm. Or maybe. . . ." He looked across the river at the bluffs, and I saw a hunger in him that was the same as mine. "Maybe keep goin' till I figure it out."

"You ever think about what's out there?"

"All the time. I've been to California. Never did figure why I came back. It's like a calling. All us Earps are that way. Itchy-footed. Can't wait to see what's over the next rise."

"You see the ocean?" That was a sight I couldn't imagine, hard as I tried.

"Can't miss seein' it. It's there. Big. Big as heaven."

I closed my eyes and tried again. Water clear to the horizon, and restless, like the river got when the wind came up or the snow melted off in the spring. Then I told him about the wagons that'd come through Ponca Bottom, and how I'd wanted to go with them so bad it like to tore me apart.

"Maybe someday we'll both go," he said.

The river had taken on the dark, and lights was shining in town, a necklace of pretty, yellow beads. He'd said "we", but I let it pass. "The stars are comin' out."

"And I better get you back or that sister of yours will think I kidnapped you."

"Don't try it." I was laughing.

He looked down at me, considering. "When we go, it'll be your choice. I never much liked carryin' porcupines around. Even the little ones."

For that, I had no smart answer. He'd said "we" again, and I sure hoped he meant it.

We went on like that a while, walking out together when he was in town. You might say we got to know each other, but I think I knew all there was to know about Virge the first time I laid eyes on him.

When he told me he was quitting the stage line and going up to Newton to farm just like he wanted, there wasn't a question of me staying behind. It was early spring. The ice was going out on the river, and you could smell it, smell the wet dirt, the sap running in the trees. For about a week the cranes had been coming in, and their crying filled me with the urge to move on, follow their path no matter where it took me.

"When are you leavin'?" I asked, knowing that no matter what he said, I was going along.

"As soon as you're ready."

That settled that. "Is tomorrow soon enough?"

He laughed, took my face in his big, rough hands. "You're sure you don't want a big church weddin' or something?"

"I ain't never been in a church in my life," I told him. "Why start now?"

"Just asking. I don't want to start off with a mistake. Not if you been dreaming about it."

"I'll tell you this," I said, looking right at him so he'd know for sure I meant it. "Where you go, I go. Now and for the rest of my life. And I don't need no blabber-mouth preacher or confessin' my sins to make it so."

He looked straight back out of those level, blue-gray eyes that never lied. "Same here. But we won't tell the folks."

"How come?"

"Methodists," he said. "All the way back."

"And I'm a heathen."

"Funny, you look like Allie Earp to me."

And that was as married as we ever wanted or needed. The one thing I never told him was what Melissa had to say when I got home and told her we was leaving. Oh, she was pleased I'd found me a good man—"None better," was how she put it. But then she gave a snicker, looked like she was going to bust.

"What's so funny?" I was getting ready to defend Virge with all I had.

"Don't get mad. It's not him. Or you. But . . . but. . . ." She went into another fit. "But you hardly come up to his middle. How're you going to . . . you know? He could squash you flat, then what?"

Well, I saw her point and fell to laughing, too, until the tears came to my eyes. It took a while before I could say anything. "You forget I worked at Mollie's. I kept my eyes open, and there's ways you wouldn't dream about. Maybe I'll just crawl on top like a grasshopper on a punkin."

At that we laughed harder, ended up hugging each other and crying some more 'cause who knew if we'd ever see each other again, ever sit together like sisters who'd shared good and bad and could laugh together about things that wasn't ever talked about.

"I'm going to miss you something awful," she said when we'd sobered up. "Promise you'll write. And if I hear from Lydie, or . . . Pa, or any of them, I'll write and tell you."

"And if you need me, I'll come runnin'."

She shook her head. "No, you won't. You stick with your man like I'm stickin' with Tom. All I want is to know how you are and where."

"I'll be just fine," I said. And for a long, long time that was the truth.

Virge and I left Council Bluffs on the stage, him driving and me sitting alongside. Melissa came to the depot to see us off. It had started to rain, lightly, but the sky promised more to come, and I'd shocked both her and Virge when I announced I was going to sit up top instead of inside with the passengers.

"Honey, you'll get wet," Virge said, looking worried.

"Or sick." That was Melissa.

"I'd a heap rather be up there instead of inside with a bunch of drunks and that farty old man," I said.

There was, for sure, a fat old man who must've filled up with beans the night before, and I'd already made sure to stand upwind from him. Virge gave in with a grin. "All right. But don't say I didn't warn you about gettin' soaked."

"Maybe it'll make me grow."

Melissa rolled her eyes. "And maybe marriage will sweeten that mouth of yours."

Virge lifted me up, still grinning. "I hope not. That's why I love her."

He'd said it, and I felt good inside. Although we'd talked, and kissed, and had our wedding night—and that wasn't near as hard as Melissa had thought—we'd not once said anything about love. It wasn't our way, either of us, but once in a while it was nice to hear. I made a note in my head to tell Virge I loved him, too, then thought better of it. The word didn't cover how I felt. It's just a sound, come to it. Still, I wish I'd said it more often, 'cause now it's 'way too late.

He climbed up on the seat, took the reins, let the brake loose. "Ready?"

My heart beat so hard it like to jumped in my mouth. I nodded, looked down at Melissa, and saw her eyes full of tears.

"Write," she whispered.

"You, too."

And then we went off at a good trot, leaving Council Bluffs, Omaha, Ponca Bottom, and my childhood behind.

Chapter Eleven

It rained, all right, but I was too excited to care. I was busy hanging onto the seat and admiring how Virge handled those horses, like they was toys instead of the big brutes they were. He could have been playing a fiddle the way his hands and fingers moved on the reins—gentle but sure, and never making a mistake.

All the Earps was good with horses. They got it from Ginnie Ann, their ma, who had a way with every animal she touched or looked at, even birds, and who could stick on a horse as good as any one of her boys.

It was wet and cold, and the wind was in our faces, but I was having an adventure, and Virge was with me, and it seemed we were flying along the road across the Iowa prairie, flying like the cranes. I wrapped my arms around my middle, huddled down next to Virge's warmth—and, my, that man was always just as warm as a good fire—and let my heart spin out across the plains.

It took a day and a night and part of the next day to cover the miles to Newton, and Virge and I had to sit inside a while when the relief driver came on.

"I'm goin' to catch some shut-eye," he said, once we was jammed in with the old man and a couple other passengers, one of 'em the worse for the bottle of whiskey he kept slugging. "You should, too."

How anybody could sleep on that hard seat, in that coach that slipped and slid and like to pounded my seat bone up through my mouth was a wonder, but in a little while Virge was snoring, leaving me wide awake with nothing to do.

I just kept looking at him and wondering how he'd come to pick me, and what kind of magic had brought us together. Everything seemed to have happened so fast, and me not thinking, really, just going along like I was caught up in a river current. What did I know about this man I'd taken for a husband beyond the fact that he was kind, honest, and tugged at me like he had a rope around my heart? I knew he'd been brought up on a farm, that he'd been in the war, that he had four brothers, a sister, and a half-brother, and that he had a way with horses. But who he was down deep couldn't be proved. Not by me.

And that got me scared. Setting there in that coach alone with what I was thinking, I realized I'd thrown in with a stranger, and what courage I'd started with leaked right out of me till I felt like a doll with no stuffing. Me! Maybe every bride has a time like I did, an hour, a day of pure panic. I don't know. I never thought to ask another woman, and by the time I had a woman friend to talk to, I wasn't scared any more, having found out that Virge was exactly like I'd thought from the beginning, and that, if ever two people was made for each other, it was us.

The coach came to a sliding stop, and Virge woke straight up. "Time to change horses. Drivers, too. You want to stay inside?"

"Not on your life," I told him. "Not even if it's blowin' a blizzard." I never did take to being jammed in with a bunch of strangers, and I'd got me a headache in spite of the cold air that blew in through the leather curtains. "I'm goin' where you go, just like I said."

Fresh horses was brought out by a man with a beard so long he could've tucked it in his belt. "Heard this was your last trip," he said to Virge.

"Yep. Going to try farmin' a while. Got a place near my Uncle Renz's."

The man spat. "Better you than me."

Virge grinned. "Now that's a fact, Milt. You aren't built right to follow a plow. That beard of yours'd get caught up and choke you."

Milt spit out a stream of tobacco juice, and looked at me. "You been robbin' the cradle?"

"Nope. This here's my bride."

"I'll be damned." He spit again, and I gave him a look that should've turned him to stone.

"You will, and that's a fact," I said.

Virge hoisted me up to the seat. "Better watch what you say, Milt. She's got a way of makin' you wish you'd shut up."

"I'll be damned," Milt said again, making me think maybe his brain was addled.

Virge climbed aboard, picked up the lines. "Stay out of trouble, Milt!" he yelled, and we was off again, the wind blowing fresh in our faces.

I started thinking about the doubts I'd had earlier, wondering if every time we met somebody he'd have something nasty to say about me looking like a little kid. "Is that going to happen every time?" I asked Virge when the road leveled off and the rain let up. "I can't help being little."

He gave me a sideways glance. "It don't bother me. Don't let it get to you. Hell, Milt don't know any better. Besides, I like you the way you are."

Well, I felt better after that, and figured I'd ask me a few more questions. "Tell me about your Uncle Renz. What's he like?"

Virge chuckled. "You might say it's on account of him we came to Iowa in the first place. He was a wild one. Got a woman in trouble back in Kentucky and figured it'd be as well to move on before he got his neck stretched. So we all came with him. Us Earps stick together. But don't worry. He's settled down. Syrine's seen to it."

"Who?"

"His second wife. You'll like her. You'll like Walt and Ellen, too. Walt's their son. We couldn't ask for better neighbors. Or better farm country, either."

Privately I wondered if womanizing ran in the family, but kept my mouth shut. Later I was glad I had. Later, it didn't make no difference.

When we pulled up in front of the depot, I was a sorry sight. "Like a wet hen," Virge said. "And there's Uncle Renz and Walt come to meet you."

I started fussing with my bonnet and my hair that was every which way, and he laughed and lifted me down. "Too late for that. Anyhow, they won't care how you look. They know what travelin's like."

But Uncle Renz, who had a deep, booming voice, noticed straight off. "Why, you're no bigger than a minute, and soakin' wet! What was Virge thinkin'? Why weren't you ridin' inside?"

"You wouldn't have, either. Not if you cared to breathe," I told him, giving the fat man and the drunk a look, and deciding to pay no attention to his comment on my size.

Renz threw back his head and gave a laugh that sounded like a rutting bull. "She might be little, but she's a tough one. Guess you got it right this time, Virge."

I didn't have time to wonder what he meant because Virge took my arm and hustled me down the street to a restaurant, with Renz and Walt close on our heels.

A cup of coffee never tasted as good as that one, nor steak and eggs, neither. I ate like I'd been starved—the food in the roadhouses was only fit for hogs—and listened while the men talked.

"Syrine and Ellen are out at the cabin," Walt told me when I'd eaten all I could hold. "They wanted to fix it up pretty for you. Dad and I hauled in a cook stove last week, so I think you'll do fine. Nothin' fancy, but you'll be out of the rain."

A house of my own! It was hard for me to take in, and all I said was: "I thank you." Then I had to laugh. "I was hopin' a good soak'd make me grow."

Renz gave another roar. "Why, gal, if you're big enough to take on Virge, you don't need to grow."

Walt said—"Now, Dad."—and I remembered the woman he'd got in trouble. Looking at Renz, full of life and himself, and with a pair of eyes that took in everything from a woman's looks to whatever else was going on, I could see how it happened. That was one other thing about the Earps, all of 'em. They was handsome and attracted women like flies. And in Wyatt's case, he hated to turn a one of 'em down. If it wasn't for him and Sadie, maybe we'd all still be together. But I can't say for sure, and, like always, I'm gettin' ahead of myself.

"I reckon I'm happy the way I am," I said, and meant it.

"You did yourself proud, Virge." Renz wiped his mustache and stood up. "Now let's get goin'. Be home afore dark if we don't dawdle."

We went in Renz's buckboard, me looking around so's

not to miss an inch of my new country. And it was pretty country, green in the rain, all the trees with new leaves sparkling, and the prairie grasses thick and bent down. Plenty of water, too, the creeks and rivers running full. I breathed in the smell of it all and near fell off the seat with happiness, knowing Virge had picked a fine place to start our life.

Renz was watching me with those keen eyes. "You look like Christmas morning."

"And feel like it. How far now?"

"Just ahead. 'Round the bend and behind the trees."

I squinted, but couldn't make out a thing. Virge reached over and took hold of my hand, as excited as I was. And then we saw it, sprouting like a mushroom right out of the ground, smoke coming out of the chimney, and a couple of hounds came to greet us, tails wagging.

"Samson and Delilah," Walt said. "I saved a pup for you. Always good to have a dog around."

"Seen any wolves?" Virge asked.

"Nope. But that don't mean they aren't here."

I shivered. We'd had plenty of wolves back home, and even the sound of them howling had scared Mum out of her wits. I remembered seeing her lift her skirt and run for home, and Frank running behind, bawling his head off just hearing one.

Two women came out of the house then, and I had no trouble figuring which was which. Renz's Syrine was tall and long-nosed, with a chin on her that told me he'd be courting trouble if he went courting anybody but her. Ellen was small, like a sparrow, and was twittering a welcome just like one.

"Come in, come in. Supper's ready, and I hope you like your new house." She grabbed my arm and steered me inside.

Syrine stood there, looking me up and down. "Well," she said after a minute, "you picked the runt of the litter this time, Virge." Then, seeing my face, she laughed. "Don't mind me, child. I always say what pops in my head."

I was wondering if every time I met an Earp they'd have something to say about my size. Hell, I couldn't help it! Wonder what they'd say if they could see me now, shrunk till you'd miss me if you passed me in the street! I doubt even Virge would recognize me. Still, all I said to Syrine was: "Me, too. And sometimes it gets me in trouble."

"Best to clear the air's my motto," she said. "Besides, Virge here needs a woman to tell him how to get on. Most men do, come to think of it."

Virge kissed his aunt on the cheek, then slapped her bottom. "You're givin' Allie the wrong idea."

She gave him a kiss back, then turned to me. "Get that wet cloak off and come sit by the fire. I swear, nobody's got a lick of sense, includin' me, lettin' you stand around half drowned. It's just we've been so excited about you comin'."

She had a good heart. So did they all. I let her take my cloak and bonnet and sat, warming my hands and that place inside that had been empty so long. Gathering my new folks around and feeling that I'd come home.

Chapter Twelve

Farming's never easy, and it wasn't for us, but we was young and tough and bred on the land. First thing, Virge and Walt went over to some Dutch fella's farm and got us a team of horses, the prettiest pair I ever saw—solid black, both of 'em—good workers and sweet-tempered, broke to ride as well as to harness. Sugar and Spice I called 'em, seeing as how I believed critters, just like folks, needed names.

Before long, Virge had a crop of punkins and corn in, and had dug me a garden that I fussed over like I'd never growed anything before. That Iowa dirt was so rich it seemed all I had to do was drop in seeds and then keep the weeds from strangling what did come up.

Sometimes I ask myself why we ever left Iowa. If we'd stayed, we'd have been fat and happy, and Virge would've had two good arms to put around me, and maybe there'd have been kids to see us into old age, instead of me sitting here at my niece Hildreth's, talking mostly to myself and wondering when the Lord's coming to take me to Virge.

If we'd stayed, I could be sitting on the porch right now, watching the sun go down on the edge of the world and listening to the quiet rising up out of the prairie. There's no quiet like it that I know of. The land sings to itself, and the singing only makes the silence deeper—crickets in the grass, a horse snorting off somewhere, 'poorwills calling down along the river, and now and then a lark flying straight up, whistling a good night. Sometimes we'd sit out there, not saying a word, just content with ourselves and what we was doing, and around us that music, the smell of rain, and in June the wild roses that spilled out flowers and perfume till I got dizzy.

We had two dogs, and they'd be laying alongside us or out hunting rabbits just for the fun of it. There was Walt's hound pup I named Royal 'cause he knew he was a prince and who we called Roy, and a shaggy sheep dog that showed up one day and decided he'd found himself a home. I called him Joe, and he stuck with us long after we'd moved on.

Sounds like paradise, and it was, even to the snakes, and there was a heap of 'em, all kinds—big, shiny black snakes, skinny, little, stripy ones, and rattlers big around as my arm. Between me and those snakes, we gave Virge hissy fits!

Then and now I never could stand wearing shoes for very long. It's the feel of dirt that I love, like I'm planted and growing, and no damned shoe leather pinching my toes or giving me blisters. When I was a kid, we never put shoes on from the first warm day till the first frost. Couldn't afford 'em in the first place, and the ones we had got handed down till there wasn't no soles left and no way to fix 'em.

"Damn it, Allie! Put on your boots!" That'd be Virge, mad as a hornet 'cause he was always scared I'd get bit. "If I come in and find you all swelled up, I'll take you over my knee whether you're hurtin' or not."

"I'm too ornery to get bit, and they know it." Oh, what a smart mouth I always had!

He knew when he was beat. In the end he went out and

got me a scatter-gun and made sure I knew how to use it.
He taught me to shoot his pistol, too, except it was near as
big as I was and heavy to boot. Still, I never aimed at something but what I hit it square, and I went around shooting
snakes and burying 'em for fertilizer.

"Got 'em all," I told Virge at the end of summer.

"Huh! There's more where those come from, and well
you know it, so don't go gettin' cocky. I don't want to lose
you, especially not to a damned rattler."

"You won't."

He picked me up and swung me around. "You put your
shoes on, and I'll take you to a party."

Lord, he knew how I loved a get-together, folks
laughing, dancing, the fiddler going at it with all his muscle,
the young folks giddy and spinning around like a flock of
birds.

"Whose? Where?" I was breathless.

"Walt's. Renz don't hold with dancin', but Ellen's ready
for some fun along with the rest of us."

I thought about that—about working sunup to sundown,
Virge in the fields or hauling and chopping wood, me at the
wash pot, the stove, in the garden, churning or baking till I
was like to drop. But even chores had a kind of fun to 'em,
like we was doing our best and glad of it.

Walt and Ellen was right too, though. There comes a
time for letting loose, visiting neighbors, for putting on your
best dress and, yes, your damned shoes, and forgetting
about work, about yesterday or tomorrow.

I clapped my hands like a kid. "I'll just take that cake I
made. And I'll have me a bath. And I promise to keep my
shoes on just so's you don't step on my feet with your big
clodhoppers and break 'em in half."

"Why, honey, you don't have to worry about me steppin'

on you," he said, laughing out loud. "I'll just pick you right up and dance you around."

"You won't, either." I was busy hauling out the washtub.

He kept on laughing, and, when we led off in the first dance, damned if he didn't lift me up and do just like he said! Far as I know, folks was still talking about it when we left Iowa. We sure were a sight!

The letter from Virge's half-brother, Newton, came about a week later. He'd been farming over in Kansas, but that year the grasshoppers had eaten near everything, and he and his family were close to starving.

Virge read the letter twice, then gave it to me. "We got to send them some of what we have. I'm damned if I'll sit here while my family goes hungry."

"We got enough to spare," I said, worried more about Newton's kids than about ourselves.

Virge went to a local freight office and we loaded a wagon with punkins, cornmeal, sugar, salt, anything we could think of. But when we were done, there was only just enough to tide us over the winter, and Virge said: "Allie, I been thinkin'. . . ."

Right then my heart sank to my toes. How'd I know what he was going to say? How'd I know our farming days were numbered? But I did. He'd been talking to the teamster about the gold that'd been discovered in the Black Hills, and both of 'em heard opportunity calling.

The run was on to a place that, before the strike, had been a miserable cañon miles from anywhere and in a country crawling with Injuns. Like cow towns, mining towns grew up overnight, with folks coming from all over, some of 'em with no more than the clothes they was wearing. And like everybody else, they had to eat. They needed supplies—flour, sugar, salt, beans and bacon, boots and coats, picks, shovels, machinery for the mines already producing. And liquor. Especially that. Miners loved their booze, and so did the whores and gamblers that came on their heels like flies to the honey pot.

What's needed then is wagons to haul the world in, and the men to drive 'em. Men like Virge who could handle a six- or eight-horse hitch. Itchy-footed men always looking over the horizon for the main chance and not scared of what they'd find.

I didn't know about any of this when Virge and I set out for Sidney, Nebraska, but I learned. Over the years I've watched more towns boom and bust than I want to think about. Deadwood was only the first. I wish it'd been the last.

Chapter Thirteen

We set out early in spring, leaving Renz and Walt to farm our place. The last thing I saw was our little house, already looking lonely and sad, and I wondered if this was what my life was going to be like, if my early years moving from one job and place to another hadn't set a stamp on me, and the same with Virge. Because the Earps was all restless, even Ginnie Ann. Seems they just couldn't stay in one place long enough to call it home or make it pay. As for me, although I longed for a place of our own, I was almost as bad, always wanting to see what was ahead, at least in those early years.

We stopped in Council Bluffs a couple days to see Melissa and Tom, and what a reunion that was! I felt like I hadn't seen them for a hundred years, could hardly talk for wanting to cry. There was a baby, too, a bright little fella. I reckoned Tom's accident hadn't hurt him any place that counted, and said as much to Melissa, who blushed red.

"How you talk!" she said, looking around to see if anybody'd heard.

"No different from anybody else."

"Different from the ladies I know."

I laughed. "Then I guess I ain't no lady."

As a matter of fact, I never gave a hoot in hell about being thought a lady. All I wanted was to be me and try not to hurt anybody while I was at it.

Melissa's big news was that she'd got a letter from Lydia who had got married and was living in Kansas. She printed the address on a scrap of paper, and I gave it to Virge to keep safe. I never had much schooling, had taught myself to read and write a little, but writing for me was always a chore.

When it came time to leave, Melissa, Tom, and the baby went to the train station with us.

"Seems like you're always goin' away," she said. "Blowin' around like one of them tumbleweeds."

"And weighin' just about as much," Virge said, kissing her cheek.

"Take care of her."

He looked at her straight. "As best I can and as much as she'll let me."

And then we were moving, leaving the river, the bluffs, and everything familiar far behind. We rode straight across Nebraska, and all we took with us was our clothes, Virge's saddle, and the dog, Joe.

"I ain't leavin' without him," I'd told Virge. "He come to us, and we took him in. It'd break his heart. Roy's different. He's better off with Walt. But Joe's comin' with us or I ain't goin', either."

So he rode in back with the baggage and the mail sacks, and the baggage fella made a pet of him, and he came through fine.

There was a late blizzard blowing when we got to Sidney, one of those wet snows that makes you feel spring's never coming, that gets right next to your skin and freezes your bones. I stood shivering while Virge got our bags and collected Joe, who didn't look any too happy at leaving the warm car.

"I guess I won't be goin' anywhere any day soon," Virge said, looking up at the sky that was just a mess of gray clouds.

"Just as well we get settled first." I wasn't looking forward to doing nothing while he went back and forth to Deadwood. It'd be the first time I was alone since we'd got hitched.

"First let's find us a hotel." He took my hand, tucked it under one arm, clicked to the dog, and we went off down the street, me fighting the drifts best I could.

Next day the sun was out, the snow was melting, and we found ourselves a two-room cabin that had belonged to a freighter who'd gone to Deadwood, got bit by the gold bug, and stayed. It wasn't much of a house, but we was lucky to get it, times being what they was. And in a couple weeks Virge was off on his first run, driving for a fella he knew from his railroad days, Pete Dawkins.

By the time he got back from his fourth trip, it was near the middle of July, and I'd had enough of being alone. "I ain't coolin' my heels here any more. I didn't get married to be a widow six months out of the year, or spend my days talkin' to a dog. When you pull out again, I'm comin' along."

He looked surprised, then grim. "Honey. . . ."

"Forget the sweet talk. Like I told you, me and old Joe's tired talkin' to ourselves."

"It's a rough trip. And the men, well, they aren't used to havin' a woman along."

"Then they'll damn' well get used to it." I laughed when a thought struck me. "What about that Canuteson woman? She drives freight and it don't seem to bother the men."

He laughed, too. "She's not exactly what they call a woman."

Madam Canuteson was famous all along the trail, for her men's clothes, her mule team, and the cussing she used to get her critters moving. My, how that woman could cuss! I heard her once down at the freight office and what came out of her mouth was impressive as hell.

"Maybe I can hitch a ride with her," I said, knowing just how Virge would take that.

"Damn it, Allie!" He was tugging at his mustache like he did when I had him buffaloed. "You . . . I . . . she's no company for you, and I can't be lookin' out for you. It's a rough haul, and the Injuns are stirred up. We promised 'em we'd stay out of that land, and now we're swarmin' over it. Anything could happen. Look what happened to Custer."

Everybody knew what had happened to Custer at the Little Big Horn just that June. I'd been on my own in Sidney when the news had come in, and it was all folks could talk about. If the Injuns were stirred up, they couldn't hold a candle to the whites who were ready to go on the warpath themselves. Vengeance and Injuns—the two words went together. But always, in some part of my mind, I remembered "my" Injuns, and Ponca Mary who'd been a good friend. The way I saw it, there was good Injuns and bad ones, same as with the rest of us. And if we'd broken a promise to them, then we had to take the consequences.

"And what if it happens to you?" I asked, getting madder by the minute. "What if you get killed, and me here waiting? How you think I'm going to feel then?"

That shook him. I reckoned it would, and he said: "I was figurin' on you and me goin' on the last run. Maybe it'll be safer then. And Morg and Wyatt'll be in Deadwood by then. We thought we might spend the winter up there."

"Well, for sure I ain't spendin' it here by myself," I said. "Nor the rest of the summer, neither."

"Not going to let up, are you?"

"Nope. There's always Madam Canuteson. Why's she call herself Madam, anyhow?"

He cocked an eyebrow. "Maybe she was one."

Now she was a big, strapping woman with a voice deep as a man's. I figured it was likely she'd been a saloon bouncer. But all I said was: "Pity her girls."

For a minute it looked like he was thinking about something else, then he said: "You got a point. I wonder what Wyatt would've made of her back in Peoria?"

It seemed to me we were losing track of my purpose, which was to get on that freight wagon with him. "What're you talkin' about now?"

"Wyatt and Morg ran a couple of houses back there. So did Jim Earp's wife, Bessie. Wyatt was broke, and it was easy money. But Bessie sure doesn't look like Canuteson. Jim wouldn't go near a woman like that."

It took me a minute to digest the fact that my brothers-in-law had owned whorehouses. Not that it mattered. I had nothing against whores. After all, Fannie had been a good friend, and Mollie back in Omaha had saved my bacon. Still, I had to ask: "What were you doin' while your brothers was pimpin' and takin' care of the ladies?"

He gave me a look that said he knew I was jealous and thought it was funny. "Tendin' bar."

"Sure," I said, wishing I could scratch the eyes out of those girls. "I bet you weren't fightin' 'em off."

"Well," he hesitated, "I hadn't met you yet."

"You've met me now."

"And I thank the Lord every day, even when you're naggin' at me."

I overlooked the nagging part. "Bullshit. You ain't a prayin' man. And what're Wyatt and Morg goin' to do in

Deadwood? Open another house?"

Virge shrugged. "Not a one of us knows what Wyatt's going to do one day to the next. He plays close to his chest. Morg . . . well, it's hard to say. Morg likes a good time. He'll do 'most anything as long as it's fun or there's money in it. He'll probably be gamblin'. Wyatt, too."

"Just tell me you won't be tendin' bar," I said. Then, knowing I had the advantage: "Just so you know, I'm leavin' here when you do, even if Joe and me have to stow away somewhere."

"God help us all," he said, giving in with a shrug. "And God help the Injuns if they get ahold of you." Then he kissed me. Hard. I never got a chance to answer, which was probably just as well.

So that's how I got to Deadwood, riding on the freight wagon pulled by six ornery mules and loving every minute of it. We passed through some of the prettiest country I ever saw. The prairie grasses was tall and heavy with seed, and in late afternoon the thunderclouds built up so high I had to bend my head back to see the tops. We'd ride in and out of their shadows that colored the sand hills blue and purple, just like somebody had tossed down a painted canvas.

Sure it was hot and hard going, just like Virge said, but the men paid me no mind, and I was having an adventure, getting my first taste of the West I'd dreamed back in Ponca Bottom. If there was Injuns, we never saw any. Probably they skedaddled after the Custer massacre and were hiding out best they could. We run across plenty of cavalry out scouting for 'em, though, most of 'em looking like they'd rather be some place else.

The Black Hills was different from Nebraska, and from any country I'd ever seen. I kept wanting to jump off the wagon and pick me some of the flowers that grew in the mountain meadows. Every place I looked was flowers—all colors, pink, yellow, blue, orange—like a sunset those meadows were, so bright it hurt to look.

One night, when I was fixing supper, Virge went out and picked an armload near as big as I was. "I figured I'd bring my girl some flowers," he said, handing them over. "They're almost as pretty as you."

That's how he was, see. Always knowing what pleased me and doing his best to give it to me. I kept that bouquet in a jug till the flowers dried up and faded, but I can still see 'em. Black-eyed Susans and coneflowers, and some I never did give names to. But no matter. They was all beautiful.

I think it was the next day that we saw a herd of buffalo off in the distance. Must've been thousands of 'em, covering the earth as far as we could see, and some of the men went off to hunt.

"Take a good look," Virge said. "You mightn't see that many again."

"Why not?"

"We're huntin' them. I've seen places that's just piles of bones and the meat left to rot. They're going just like the Injuns, and I'm sorry."

"Why leave the meat?" I asked. "Ain't it good?"

"The best. But they're huntin' hides. That's where the money is. Last I heard, there's men shootin' them off the trains just for the hell of it. And when they're gone, the Injuns'll be gone, too, or on reservations, livin' off what we give them."

Something twisted in me at the thought of all that slaughter, and mostly for nothing. But I didn't even try to say what I was thinking. It was too hard getting the words out for what I felt. But I watched that herd till it disappeared behind a row of hills and never have forgot it.

That night I got my first taste of buffalo meat, and thought it was a shame not to find some way to use it. The Injuns dried it and made jerky. It kept all winter. Us whites, though, seemed always to be in a hurry, never taking the time to do things right. There's lots to be said for moving slow, learning what's around, making do with what's there.

Virge and me and a couple others were sitting around the fire, enjoying our supper. Stars were coming out, and the air smelled of wood smoke, roasting meat, and the sharp scent of the pine trees that covered the hills.

I said, for no special reason: "It's no wonder the Injuns don't want us here."

One of the men snorted. "And we don't want them here, neither. Damned redskins think they own the place."

"Seems to me like they did," I said.

"Murderin' bastards ain't fit to live. Beggin' your pardon."

I didn't answer. But then and now there's a piece of me that's sorry for those Injuns. The West was paradise, and they got kicked out or killed just like the buffalo, as if there wasn't no difference between 'em. I got up, gathered the supper plates, and went to wash 'em off in the creek that ran along one side of the camp. Old Joe came with me and lay in the grass to watch.

"Well," I said to him, "what do you think? Are they murderin' bastards, or are we?"

He was wore out from chasing every critter he run across from jack rabbits to spindly-legged antelope, and all he did was thump his tail.

"You talkin' to yourself?" Virge had followed us.

"Thinkin' out loud."

In the dark, he looked bigger than life, and solid, like one of the pines. "I'm goin' to bed. Don't think too long."

84

Well, I knew what he meant and what he wanted, 'cause I wanted the same. There was always that pull between us, never talked about, just there.

"Guess I'm done thinkin'," I said. "My brain's wore out. For tonight anyhow."

I lay awake a long time after. A little piece of moon hung in the West, and an owl was hooting in the trees. I lay there, counting my blessings and knowing I was maybe the happiest, luckiest woman in the world.

Virge had made us a bed in the wagon so I wouldn't have to sleep on the ground and so we'd have some privacy. And when it rained, me and Joe would crowd in and sit, and wonder about what was in all those sacks and barrels.

There was onions. I could tell that much with my nose. And potatoes, and coffee, and barrels of salt pork and flour. Bolts of cloth, good, hard-wearing stuff, and boots in all sizes, and barrels of what passed for whiskey. I tried to make a list, and Virge laughed when he saw it.

"You forgot the blasting powder."

"What?" I damned near jumped out and ran.

He caught the hem of my skirt. "I was joking. The powder's in the last couple wagons."

"We could get blown to flinders!"

He laughed. "Don't worry. It won't happen. Not unless somebody gets careless. But don't say I didn't warn you about comin' along."

I stood there on my two feet, glaring at him. "Virgil Earp, Injuns don't bother me. I can handle Injuns. They're like us, only starvin', and besides, they ain't bulletproof. A bunch of horny teamsters don't worry me, neither. Blasting powder's different."

"It is. That's a fact. But it's what's needed, and we haul it. We don't have a choice."

As far as I was concerned, everybody has a choice. "You don't have to be a teamster," I told him. "Why . . . you might even be President."

He laughed so hard he clutched his belly. "Oh, Lord, Allie, can't you see us? You barefoot, and me in my muddy boots? We're just plain folks, honey. We'd get laughed out."

"Lincoln was plain folks, too," I reminded him. "Look what he done."

"But not like us. He took to politics."

I pondered on that for a long while. Weeks. Thinking plain made me forget about that damned blasting powder. Finally I came to the conclusion that we was as good as the next, and nobody was going to tell me different. Not Virge, not nobody. And if I damned well took it in my head to sit in the White House, I'd do it.

Well, I was young. Foolish. Even ignorant. But I'll say this. Me . . . and the Earps . . . all of us never bowed our heads to nobody and were damned proud of it.

Chapter Fourteen

Deadwood was booming, all right. Cabins, stores, saloons were going up as fast as the logs were cut, and the hills all around was covered with tents that served as home for the prospectors and miners who hadn't yet struck anything but rocks and dirt. The day we pulled in there was an angry mob crowding the main street. I wondered what they was so riled up about, and soon found out. My old friend, Jim Hickok, known by then as Wild Bill, had been shot in the back while playing poker, and the son-of-a-bitch that shot him, Jack McCall, had been tracked down and put in the cooler.

"Jim didn't deserve to die like that," I said to Virge. "He was a good man. Nice, even to us kids."

"McCall's a damned coward. I expect he'll get hung."

"Hangin's too good for him." I fought down anger and sorrow for the man I'd known, the man who'd done his best for so many people. "He oughta be cut in pieces and fed to the hogs."

Every time I got good and mad, it tickled Virge for a reason I couldn't understand. He was grinning in spite of the death of a good man.

"Why're you laughin'? The son-of-a-bitch deserves what

he gets, and you just said it, so what's so funny about what *I* said?"

"Nothing."

"There is, too, or you wouldn't be laughin'."

"Honey, you can get madder faster than anybody I ever saw," he said finally. "Little as you are, you're downright dangerous, especially when you got that shotgun handy."

That tickled me. Dangerous was I? Well, good! Women have it hard enough, and little women even harder. We've got to fight just to keep up.

"You remember that," I said with a grin.

"Every day. And I'll be sure and warn Wyatt and Morg. I'd hate to lose one of my brothers."

"How soon do you think they'll get here?"

He shrugged. "Sometime before the snow flies. Once that happens, it's not an easy trip. We could get snowed in and stay that way from what I hear."

I looked up and down the gulch. Main Street was clogged with wagons, drays, horses, mules, ox teams, and folks on foot, and it did come to me that living in Deadwood, summer or winter, might be tricky. "We better make sure we got enough to eat to last us in that case."

Now, it's been said that I could see the future, but that's not so and never was. What I had was what any farm kid had—common sense. A hard winter in that out-of-reach cañon meant a lot of folks was going to starve or freeze to death. I made up my mind it wasn't going to be us.

"Next trip, fill about half a wagon with truck for us just in case," I told him. "Take the money I been savin' from your pay and use it."

He turned that over in his mind. "Not a bad idea. We can always turn a profit on what we don't use."

He thought it was such a good idea he bought our wagon and a six-horse team, an outfit he and his brothers put to good use. Along with the grub, he brought in some laying hens and half a dozen cats, and I let out a squeak at the sight of 'em, never being partial to cats.

"What in hell are they for?"

"As many rats and mice as are here, they'll go fast."

They did, too. A couple of whores bought the prettiest ones and even named 'em. But I bet they didn't last the winter when it came. All told, though, we made $60 off those critters, which just goes to show what a smart man can do.

About the chickens, I was sure the coyotes'd get them, but we kept 'em in crates, covered 'em up in the snow, and never lost a one except to the cooking pot.

They buried Jim Hickok in the little cemetery up on Mount Moriah. A lot of folks went to the burying, knowing they'd seen the last of an honest man. That's where I first laid eyes on Calamity, a female every bit as tough as Madam Canuteson, and spitting mad. Seems she'd come into Deadwood with Hickok and his friend, Charlie Utter, and, from the way she hollered and carried on, it was plain to see she'd been in love with Jim.

Well, hell! I reckoned he was easy to love, but her? There's no telling what was going on in that head of hers—some kind of fairy tale I reckoned. Probably Hickok had been kind to her, and she took it wrong. I never did find out the truth of it all, but at McCall's trial she swore up and down that she'd chased McCall into the butcher shop where he'd hid out and had gone after him with a meat cleaver. Watching her, I figured she probably had, probably would've used it, too. She was that kind of woman and big and strong. Nobody paid her any mind, her being so odd, although I had to feel sorry for someone so damned unlovable. I figured that somewhere under her men's clothes and dirty face was feelings just like all of us women had, and I pitied her for it.

Jack McCall's no-good friends got him off, and he cut and run out of town. I'd have liked to have gone after him with a cleaver myself. Better yet with a shotgun. Lord knows I've seen enough injustice in my life, seen the law twisted or plain ignored by men calling themselves officers of the law. Every time I even think of that sack of shit Johnny Behan and his cronies I'd like to puke. But McCall's so-called trial was the first time I came face to face with evil and how the truth could get changed around by a pack of lies.

"This ain't right," I said to Virge. "There's Jim in his grave, and the one who did it free as a bird and likely to kill somebody else."

Virge looked somber. "The West has some growin' up to do. We know there's right and wrong, but there's those who don't give a damn about the right of it. All they care about's themselves and linin' their own pockets."

"What about that poor woman?"

"Calamity?" He shrugged. "She'll make out, I reckon. But I don't believe for a minute there was anything between her and Hickok. I mean, use your eyes."

"No matter. She's hurtin'."

"Can't be helped. She's not the first to lose somebody, and she won't be the last." Then he saw my face all worried and put an arm around my shoulders. "Cheer up. I'm not dead yet, and I don't have any intention of dyin' before time."

"Better not," I mumbled. But I was feeling black inside, like I had a share of every woman's heartache, and the fact that the sun had set and shadows were gathering in the cañon didn't help.

"I found us a place," he said. "That oughta cheer you up. Come on and see what you think."

We'd been living in the wagon while we looked for a place big enough for all of us. Houses was scarce, what with folks coming in by the wagonload, and we'd not found anything that suited.

"Right now a chicken coop'd look fine," I said.

It was up the gulch a ways in a side cañon—three rooms, a little space for a yard, and a shed, but it looked good.

"We'll have to chink these logs and add a room on, but that won't take long once Wyatt and Morg get here," Virge said. "I don't think you ladies'll want to share your bedrooms."

Now he hadn't told me anything about ladies, or bedrooms, neither, and I stared at him, not understanding.

"Wyatt's bringin' Mattie, and Morg's got himself hitched, too. You'll have plenty of company."

I didn't say what I was thinking, which was that three women snowed in and restless mightn't get along and winter could be hell on wheels for all of us. But I figured I'd wait and see, and later was glad I did.

Us women formed a bond in those months that never broke. There was a likeness between us, just like there was a likeness in the Earp men. We all did what we had to, held up our heads no matter what, kept on going when it seemed like the whole world was against us and we mightn't live till morning.

I'm the only one left. The one who knows their secrets, their weaknesses, their strengths. I'm the one left to tell their stories.

Chapter Fifteen

They was all coming in on the stage, and I'd near worked myself to death sweeping out that house and making sure I'd cooked enough for supper. Winter hadn't set in yet, although we'd had a couple of snow falls, but the larder was full thanks to the load Virge had brought, and, thank the Lord, there were those chickens.

"They'll be tired and hungry, and they ain't goin' to call me stingy first thing," I told Virge. "You go kill me a chicken, and I'll do the rest."

Well, he hemmed and hawed, seeing as he'd named every one. It was kind of like those hens was his children, and watching them follow him around was enough to make a dead man laugh, all those heads bobbing, and the old rooster sitting there like he was too good to join in.

Now the Earp boys have been called killers, and they was when they had to be, but seeing Virge standing there in the snow worried about killing a chicken for supper, nobody would've called him anything but a kind man. I stood firm, though. After all, I was meeting his brothers for the first time, and their wives, too. And women can get catty over the littlest thing. Nobody was going to say I didn't know how to set a good table. Besides, I never forgot the welcome Renz's family had given to me.

It took some persuading on my part, but Virge finally came back in, holding a chicken by her feet. "Damn it, Allie, she flew up on the roof right after I chopped off her head."

"They'll do it every time," I said, taking pity on him. "Give it here. I'll do the pluckin'."

He looked relieved. "I'm goin' down to the depot and wait for 'em."

"Bring 'em straight back. No showin' off the sights."

"They'll see 'em soon enough, and you stop fussing. It's only my brothers."

"I want them to like me."

He stopped at the door and turned around. "Why wouldn't they?"

"How do I know?" I was standing there, holding that bloody chicken and feeling like I was an orphan again. Silly, maybe, but that's how it was.

"They'll love you same as I do. I've known Mattie since Peoria. She's got a temper, but she's a good sort. As for Lou, if Morg picked her, she'll be fine." He chuckled. "We've all got an eye for a good-lookin' woman, but I got the best of them."

"Oh, go on!" I flapped my hands at him, and that damned chicken flew out of my grip and slid across the floor, leaving a trail of blood.

He laughed so hard he held onto his belly. "That's my girl. And I promise I won't mention how you mopped up the floor with supper."

He was out the door and gone before I could say a word, but I could hear him laughing all the way down the gulch.

Now there's something I've got to say here. Something that's stuck in my craw since that writer fella read it to me. And that is that I never, not in all my born days, greeted

Wyatt Earp by sticking a bare foot in his face! And the place I first laid eyes on Wyatt wasn't Dodge, it was Deadwood. And let me remind you, it was winter and damned cold, and I'd had my boots on for some months. Getting frostbit wasn't my idea of having fun.

My mouth might run away with me now and then, and I never had much schooling, as I said, but Mum brought us up to be mannerly and behave ourselves, and I never saw any reason to do otherwise. There's nobody on this earth who'd be impressed by the sight of a person's foot stuck out in place of a hand. And I wanted to impress not only Wyatt but the rest. So here and now I'm setting the record straight.

I told that young fella, too. I said: "I never did such a thing in my life. What crazy notion put that in your head?"

He showed his teeth in a fake smile. "I thought it would add color. Make your character more interesting."

What I said then was plain as those teeth of his. I said: "You fiddled with my character along with everything else. I'll sue the ███-damn' pants off you. My character's mine, not yours, and, far as I'm concerned, it's colorful enough the way it is."

The funny part is that he just went on reading like I hadn't said a word. Went on and on like that damned preacher at Mum's funeral. There's men like that. So full of themselves they never see what's inside another person and don't much care. Piss ants is what they are, crawling around and making pests of themselves. I never did figure why the Lord made ants—or snakes, neither. But then, I've got away from my story again.

Like I said, I'm old. But I remember like yesterday seeing the Earps come up the path and hearing a woman's laughter that sounded like little bells. I took off my apron, washed my hands quick in the basin, patted down my hair, and went to the door. Although I was smiling, my heart was beating so hard it like to have choked me. That was the first time I saw the three Earp boys together. Watching them come toward me, I saw the danger in 'em. Not that they went looking for trouble, never that, but, if it came, they'd face it down and be damned. Like a bunch of young stud horses they were, all power and grace hidden under laughter and easy ways. And just as I was taking that in, and how proud I was being Virge's wife and a part of such a family, Virge looked up and saw me, and his grin split his face from ear to ear.

"Here she is!" His voice echoed back off the hills. "Here's my lovin' bride!"

Wyatt left off whatever he'd been saying and came up to me, smiling. But I'll say this. I was glad I had nothing to hide because those eyes of his looked straight to my back-bone even while he was sticking out his hand.

"Why, Virge," he said over his shoulder, "how'd you find her? She's no bigger than a flea."

I put my hand in his, not scared any more, just a little bit put out on account of that remark about the flea, and said: "I can bite like one, too."

That broke the ice right then, and one of the women laughed out loud, that silvery sound I'd heard before. I looked past Virge and Wyatt and saw damned near the most beautiful woman I'd ever laid eyes on.

Morg wasn't as laid back as Wyatt. He grabbed me and gave me a squeeze. "Don't let Wyatt fret you. He doesn't mean anything by it. I'm Morg, and this here's Louisa."

"Loo-eye-sa." I repeated the name just like he said it, and she laughed again.

"There's no accounting for how you say it, but it's me.

And I hope you haven't gone to a lot of trouble for us." She was polite, too. Nothing beats good manners.

"We're family. No trouble at all."

All this time Mattie had been hanging back like she was shy or as scared as I'd been just a few minutes before. Well, she couldn't hold a candle to Lou as far as being beautiful, but she had a nice face, and the way she was holding onto Wyatt told me all I needed to know about her.

"You're Mattie," I said. "And you must be worn to a nub after bouncin' around in that stagecoach."

"Feels like we been on the road forever." It came out a whisper. "But it's good bein' here."

"And let's get inside, instead of standin' out here in the cold." Virge threw open the door and gave me a wink. "Not so bad, was it?"

"It was fine. I like them."

"Told you." He gave me a smack on the rear.

"Here, now," Morg said. "No foolin' around allowed. Or horseplay, either. Least not till dinner's over."

At that the three men hooted and doubled over like a bunch of bad kids, leaving us women to wonder what had got into them.

When they sobered up, Virge explained. "We used to go at it after supper. Turned over the table, dishes and all, and fought it out with Ma eggin' us on. Mostly for the fun of it. Right, Morg?"

"Yeah. And since I was next to youngest, I caught most of it."

Like I said, for all their reputation, at times they was still rowdy boys who needed a pinch of discipline. I put my hands on my hips and scolded. "There'll be no breakin' my dishes tonight or any other night. Nor whuppin' each other, neither. First one starts, buys new dishes and gets to wash 'em." But I was smiling, so they'd know I was joking.

"Atta girl," Virge said. "You tell us."

"I just did. Now let's get your coats off. There's hot coffee, and supper's nearly done. Who's hungry?"

Together Virge and Wyatt said: "Morg."

Morg slapped his belly. "All the time. You'd think Ma never fed me."

Later I found out why they all fell to laughing again. Ginnie Ann was one of the best cooks ever. If anybody starved at her table, it was 'cause they was sick and off their feed to begin with. But that's how I met Wyatt, Morg, Lou, and Mattie, and the friendships that we made in Deadwood lasted until death took everybody. Everybody but me.

Chapter Sixteen

The men got a job cutting and hauling timber and cordwood and was gone sunup to sundown, but the money was coming in, and we was saving it, seeing as we didn't need to buy much grub. Fact is, Virge and me was smarter than we knew, 'cause along in September General Crook and his troops had come into Deadwood worn down from chasing Injuns they'd never even seen, let alone caught. Their clothes was in rags, their horses, what ones they hadn't eaten, was gaunted, and the men starving. So what they did was buy up all the food in town and be damned to the rest of the folks.

Virge went down to the Langrishe Theater to hear Crook give a speech, saying as how the Injuns was all going to be caught and put back on the reservation, and how we'd all be protected from attack come hell or high water.

"Smoke blowin'," Virge said. "He's been out there all summer, chasin' his own tail. There'll be plenty of Injun trouble before it's over, and them and Deadwood's in for a damned hard winter."

He was right about that. Soon after came the blizzards and the cold that like to blistered the skin clean off a person. The place was snowed in and the world was snowed out, and I reckon there was a number who froze to death right in their tents and who wasn't found till spring. Before that, though, two more who figure in my story blew into town.

First I heard was late one afternoon when Wyatt came in from making a delivery. He was stamping his boots and rubbing his hands together. "I just met Doc Holliday getting off the stage," he said. "Is there enough supper to go around?"

"Who?" us three women asked at once.

"An old friend. And his woman. And I'd be grateful, Mattie, if you don't open up old sores."

Mattie squared her jaw. She could be stubborn as the worst mule, a habit that didn't set well with Wyatt, although he hadn't said anything. "Her?"

"Yeah. But she's Doc's problem now. Not yours or mine."

"As long as she stays that way."

"Who're we talkin' about?" I asked. "And sure we got enough for supper."

"Big Nose Kate," Mattie snapped at me. "Some foreign whore."

That was the pot calling the kettle black the way I saw it, but saying that would've probably set her off. "She ain't whorin' now, is she?" I asked. "Anyhow, it ain't up to us to talk about how she made a livin'." To Wyatt I said: "Bring 'em on. We got plenty. And we all know how to be polite."

He gave me a grateful look. "Thanks. I owe Doc. I'll go round 'em up."

When he'd gone, I looked at Mattie. "You look like a horse with a burr up its tail. Suppose you tell Lou and me what's goin' on so we don't stick our feet in our mouths."

She started pacing the floor. "I was back on the farm

with the folks. Wyatt was in Wichita, workin' as a cop. And she was workin' at Bessie's!"

By this time I knew Bessie was Jim Earp's wife and as good a madam that ever worked. Although I knew she'd blow up, I said it: "The pot callin' the kettle black?"

Sure enough, Mattie turned on me, her eyes like slits. "You don't know, so shut up! Just shut up or I'll. . . ."

"What?" I was holding an iron skillet, and I hefted it higher. Be damned if I'd let her get the better of me.

She backed off, knowing I'd brain her. "Nothin'. Never mind. I just get so damn' mad thinkin' about him and her. Together. And me workin' myself to death on that farm. I'd had enough of farmin'."

"I had a man tell me once they're all dirty old men one time or another. Wyatt ain't a saint. None of 'em are."

She looked at me with tears in her eyes. "I want to be the only one. Don't you see?"

At that point Lou gave a snort. "Oh, honey, men are men, and the Earps more than most. Just be glad for what you got. I am."

Well, she and Morg were a loving pair like Virge and me. About Wyatt and Mattie I wasn't so sure. There was a restlessness in him, and I got the feeling he was just marking time, putting up with Mattie 'cause he didn't know what else to do. Looking back, I see I was right, and I reckon Mattie knew it even then.

Old Joe started whining like he always did when the men was coming, and I put my arm around Mattie. "Dry your eyes and hold your head up. This here's your house, too, so don't show her nothin' but good manners. You hear?"

She sniffed. "You have the most sense."

"I come by it the hard way."

Lou opened the door, and I got my first look at Doc and

Kate, seeing right off that he was ailing and that she was a cut above any whore I ever met, and better dressed, too, in a coat with a fur collar and a hat with velvet ribbons wide as my hand.

As far as her nose went, I never could figure how she came by her moniker. She had a long nose for a fact, but it fit her face fine, and her face was maybe not beautiful but it surely was handsome. And proud. She always carried herself like she was Queen of England, not out of snobbishness but just 'cause it was born in her.

To tell the truth, I could see her and Wyatt together. They was cut from the same mold, sure of themselves and easy with it, not like Mattie who always reminded me of a mutt hoping for a pet, then sulking when it didn't come.

"Thank you so much for asking us to dinner," Kate said to me when Wyatt had introduced them all around. "It's kind of you."

I thought with a voice like hers—husky and just a bit foreign, like Mattie said—she could charm the pants off any man, 'specially in the dark. With that in my mind, I grinned at her.

"Can't have friends wanderin' around with their stomachs growlin'," I said. "Life here's hard enough as it is." And was surprised when she grinned back, cat-like, her eyes sparkling.

"Good company makes life happy." She was going to say more, but Doc started coughing, a terrible sound like he was bringing up his insides, and the shine went straight out of her, replaced by what looked like fear.

He was a lunger. I saw it plain and figured he'd be lucky to live out the winter. Well, I was wrong about that. He lasted another ten or so years, but I wouldn't have bet on it that night. I got out the whiskey bottle and mixed him what

Mum had always called a toddy.

He drank it straight down like a man used to drinking, and smiled. "It won't cure me, but it sure helped. Thanks."

He wasn't afraid of dying. I could see that. He didn't want to, but he'd got used to the fact and just kept going.

"Any time," I told him. "Now, why don't you sit by the stove? Gettin' chilled ain't goin' to help that cough."

He pulled up a chair and sat watching while I fussed with the stew and Lou and Mattie put out plates. Kate came to stand beside me, curious about what was cooking.

"Deer stew," I told her. "Morg got lucky last week and shot a buck. A good thing, too. We're tryin' to spare the chickens as long as we can."

She sniffed the steam rising out of the kettle and laughed. "In Hungary there is a saying . . . 'When a peasant eats chicken, either the peasant or the chicken is sick.' "

That didn't make sense to me, so all I said was: "Hungary?"

"Where I was born. Someday, maybe, I'll make *gulyaš* for you."

"She might not be good at much, but she can cook," Doc said.

We both turned and stared at him, me in surprise and Kate mad as all get out. I saw she had a temper, too, although she knew how to control it.

"And you might be skinny, but you eat like a pig," she said, looking daggers at him.

There's some folks who just can't help sniping at each other, and that's how those two were. There was love between 'em, but that wasn't enough. Both of 'em wanted more. Maybe, if Doc had been healthy, things would've gone better, or maybe not. Both had been dropped into a life they wasn't prepared for and took their troubles out on each other is how I'd put it. But I'll give her this. She stuck with him, did what she could to save him, and, when that didn't work, she was with him to the end. Loyal she was, and always with that pride and determination. Mattie could've learned from watching her, but then we are what we are.

Chapter Seventeen

The winter of 1876 was the worst I ever lived through. Blizzard followed blizzard, and Deadwood was snowed in and under. Nobody came, nobody left. Leaving was committing suicide, but staying was near as bad 'cause supplies, except for liquor, was running out. Worse than the snow was the cold. It sneaked in through cracks in the log walls and under the door, and we women huddled around the stove most of the time, trying to keep warm.

The men went out, though, still cutting timber, not for houses but for firewood, and most of it wet so that it smoked and stunk up the whole town. Our house smelled, too, of wet overcoats and the boots that sat alongside the stove, trying to dry out before they got put on again.

Lou, Mattie, and me was piecing a quilt, and that kept us busy. Kate would come up in the afternoons while Doc was trying his luck in the gambling halls. She didn't sew, but said she'd cook while the rest of us bent over the quilt that was keeping us warm as well as occupied.

I'd never known a woman who couldn't sew, and, when I remarked on it, she gave her little cat smile and shrugged. "When I was growing up, we had servants. A seamstress, too. Now it's too late for me to learn."

Lou sat back in her chair, her eyes big as saucers. "Tell

us about where you came from," she urged. "Tell us about when you were little."

Kate rubbed her hands together. She had long, slender fingers, but they was chapped and red from cold like all of ours. "Sometimes I think about Hungary," she began. "But it's better not to remember too much. We had a big house that was always warm, and servants to keep the stoves going. My mother was beautiful, and my papa was handsome, and it seems that we laughed all the time, all of us, my brothers and sisters, too. And the food! Oh, my! The cakes, the pastries! Why we weren't all fat, I don't know. And then one day it all changed."

Even Mattie was listening, although she kept her eyes on her lap and probably would've died rather than admit she was interested.

Kate went on. "It was arranged for us to come to Mexico with the new Emperor Maximilian. My papa was a doctor, a man of science, and he was excited over what he thought would be a great adventure. Mama wasn't happy. Life in Mexico was hard, and there was another baby. She was glad to leave when the revolution started, but it was too late for her. We got to Iowa, and she died. My papa, too. I was sixteen, and there were my brothers and sisters. Orphans."

"I expected they farmed you kids out," I said, knowing only too well how that was.

She shuddered. "Yes. But the man who took me tried to rape me. I stabbed him with a pitchfork and ran away because I thought I killed him. Maybe I did."

"I hope so," I said. "The bastard."

Her blue eyes were hard as glass. "Me, too. He deserved it. But I was frightened, afraid they'd come and take me to jail. So I ran away and changed my name. You know how it is to be running? All the time looking behind to see if they come after you? You know how it feels to be alone in a strange place?"

The three of us sat there not saying a word, caught up in her tragedy, and I guess she knew we understood just 'cause of our silence.

"I met Doc in Saint Louis." She gave her cat smile again. "I leave much out because to remember hurts, and because I did things I'm not proud of, but I met Doc and loved him. Then we had a fight, and I went to Wichita alone and with no money. I . . ."—she looked at us like she was deciding something—"I went to work at Bessie's."

I thought that Bessie had sure got around in this bunch, but all I said was: "Losin' your family's hardest of all."

"I lost my son."

Mattie gave a gasp. "You had a son?"

Kate turned away and stirred the pot, probably hiding tears. "I did. And, no, he wasn't Wyatt's. He died in Saint Louis of the yellow fever, and his father right after. And now you see me with no servants, no child, and a man who is dying and hates me for it."

We sat a minute before Lou said: "I ran away, too. With my sister. We didn't have to, but we wanted to see the world, get away from the farm. It wasn't how we thought, though. We got work in a Harvey House, and that was fun but hard, and strict. I didn't mind, but my sister hated rules and the Harvey House in Topeka had lots of them. She started sneakin' out at night and got in trouble. I talked her into goin' home, but I stayed on. I'd already met Morg, see." She was blushing, her cheeks the color of pink roses just from talkin' about him. Lord, but that was a love match! "I did some things I'm not proud of, either," she added, "but now I've got Morg. And two sisters." She

106

reached out her hands to Mattie and me, then beckoned to Kate. "Make that three sisters."

We sat holding hands and smiling at each other for a couple minutes, thinking. Now I can't tell what was going on in their heads, but a happiness overtook me. I was a part of a family and I had sisters, friends to share things with like I'd shared with Melissa and Lydia. It seemed I'd come full circle, and I was content.

"Me and my sister, Sara, ran away, too," Mattie said, squeezing my hand with her big one. "If you knew my ma and pa, you'd know why. We worked sunup to sundown, never had enough to eat, and got beat whenever Ma thought we did something wrong, which was all the time. There was no livin' with her, so we left. Went to Fort Scott where we thought we had relatives, but nobody knew them, and we were stuck with no place to go and no money. Sara went back home, but I'd rather have died than face Ma, and it was just as well. They married Sara off to some old fella, sayin' she'd been spoiled and wasn't good enough for a decent man, and I stayed, hopin' I'd find work. I was standin' in the street, not knowing what to do, when a woman come up to me and said she'd give me work. I was dumb, I guess. As dumb as the rest of her girls. We worked, all right. We didn't have a choice. And then one day Wyatt come in." She gave a smile at Lou. "I fell in love right then, just like you. Couldn't wait for the times he came back. He was drivin' freight from Lamar, and he'd come in and we'd talk, and, when he left, I felt like dyin'."

Kate said something in a language none of us understood, but from the sound of it she was cussing, although whether she was cussing Wyatt or Mattie, or the way women got themselves ruined, it was hard to say.

"Speak American!" Mattie snapped at her.

"Hush!" Lou said, patting Mattie's hand. "Go on. Tell the rest."

"Tell her to keep quiet, then."

"No man is worth dying for is what I said." Kate got up and went back to the stove and stirred the pot. "We have to care for ourselves."

"Easy for you to say."

Kate gave Mattie a long, level look. "No," she said. "It isn't easy. But I learned, and so will you, I hope. Now go on and finish, and I promise to keep quiet."

"There's not much more to tell. I guess I nagged at him, begged him to take me with him to Lamar, and he did. He never said nothin' about lovin' me, but I was so grateful, I kept my mouth shut. Just did for him best I could. And when he had to get out of Lamar fast, I went along."

Lou was sitting on the edge of her chair. "Why'd he have to run?"

For the first time ever, Mattie looked bright-eyed. "Him and me went and stole some horses. And when we got caught, I lied about it and got us off. After that, seein' as we were both guilty, he kind of had to take me along."

Now, I couldn't see her stealing horses or anything else, either. "You're makin' this up."

She giggled. "I'm not. He was broke, and there was all those horses runnin' loose down in the Nations. It was easy. Till he got caught. And then, after I lied for him, I told him he had to take me along with him. That I couldn't stay in town by myself after what we done. And there's never been anybody else for me. It's like without him I'm not really here." Her shoulders slumped, and she glared at Kate. "But it's not like that for *him*."

Kate's eyebrows went up in two straight lines. "It doesn't matter any more what happened between us," she said. "Hold your head up, child. Remember who you are."

"I don't know." Mattie sounded as blank as her face. "I'm tellin' you, I don't know who I am without him."

"Then you better find out," Kate said.

I went back to stitching, wondering how it felt to be a person only if you had a man to cling to. Far back as I could remember, I'd known myself. Had to or get tromped on. There we sat—four women, orphans, runaways, and at least two of us whores. We'd all seen hard times and misery, but we'd come through. If the Earp men was tough, we women was tougher. Excepting Mattie.

"Child," Kate had called her, and she was right. There was a blank space in her that needed filling, but she had no more idea how to do that than I knew how to do it for her. But right then and there I vowed I'd look out for her. She sure needed it. The rest of us would survive or be damned.

Chapter Eighteen

By the time the spring thaw came, we were all hot to get out of Deadwood, especially me. Another year in that damned dark cañon might've finished me off. I was a child of the prairie, of open spaces, and never did take to being closed in, although I didn't complain. It wouldn't have done any good if I had.

The one thing that came out of that time was that we had money in our pockets. The wood business was as good as a gold claim, and so was gambling. There was a lot of prospectors whose gold ended up at our house thanks to the Earp boys' luck at cards. Doc didn't come off too bad, either, and we had a good laugh the day Kate came in all fussed and carrying a couple sacks of gold Doc had won at the tables.

"You have to help!" She plunked the sacks down on the table, and threw her hat down alongside. "Doc says I have to sew all this in my skirt bottom to keep it safe. Hell, it must weigh ten pounds!"

I hefted it. "More like twenty."

Wyatt, who'd been on his way out and stopped to see what had Kate in such a fuss, said: "Doc's scared of those stage robbers who been workin' out of here. Tell him not to fret. I just got a job riding shotgun on one. Two of us on the stage and a rider front and back."

It was the first any of us heard of his plans, but he'd already got a rep as a sort of gunslinger from Wichita and Dodge City. Matter of fact, Seth Bullock, who was unofficial sheriff in Deadwood, had tried to hire Wyatt as a deputy, but Wyatt said he was making a lot more hauling wood.

Kate shot him a look that said she'd just as soon trust her own luck, and I thought that the sparks really must've flown between the two of 'em back in Wichita. But all she said was: "I'll do it, anyhow. Except I can't sew."

Lou took over. "We can do it. We'll make a double lining and pour the gold in."

"What we do for money." Kate sat and plunked her elbows on the table alongside the sacks.

"We know what it's like not havin' any," I reminded her. "And Doc worked for that gold."

"Worked! Taking money from fools isn't work. Doc's a dentist and a good one."

"And most folks'd just as soon die as go to one," I said. "Me included."

That husky laugh of hers spilled out. "It's the truth. You always say the truth and make us see it."

"There's no hidin' from it, is there?"

"No." Her mouth twisted. "No, damn it! Now, start sewing."

We stitched her a fake hem and a money belt to tie around her waist, and then started packing. Wyatt got us all tickets on the stage he was riding on, and all of us went as far as Cheyenne together. After that, we split and wasn't all together again until Tombstone.

Doc and Kate headed for Denver. Morg and Lou took the train to Utah, then headed up to Montana, and Wyatt went back to Dodge to take a job on the marshal's force again. Mattie went with him. Dumb as she was, I thought she loved Wyatt. Maybe if she'd been smarter, she wouldn't have hung onto him so hard that she run him out. But that's gettin' ahead of my story.

Virge and me headed for his folks' place on the farm in Rice County, Kansas. He'd had a letter from his pa saying he was tired of fighting cold weather and blizzards and was headed back to California. As soon as Virge told me that, I knew what would happen next.

"You ain't foolin' me one bit," I told him. "Sayin' you want to visit your folks. You've got it in your head to go along."

He pulled on his mustache and watched me close. "Might be a good thing. And I sure wouldn't mind some of that California weather."

After a winter in Deadwood, I was inclined to agree. "Why didn't you say so in the first place then? I'm ready."

He gave a whoop. "You're sure?"

"I said so, didn't I?"

Grabbing my arm, he said: "Come on. I know where there's a damn' good Studebaker wagon and four horses for sale, and my money's burnin' a hole in my pocket."

We drove that big wagon to Rice County, me asking questions all the way, and wondering what the rest of Virge's family would be like. His half-brother, Newton, had been farming there for a couple years. It'd been to him we sent the wagon full of provisions, and it sounded like he and his wife, Jennie, was just as fed up with farming as the old folks. For sure Wyatt was. He'd spent 1873 back there farming after he got run out of Illinois, and hated every minute of it.

The summer of 1874 was when Wyatt really got into

lawing. He didn't want any part of putting in another crop, so he followed his brother Jimmy down to Wichita, leaving Mattie behind with his folks. That's where he met Kate and took up with her till Mattie came down and busted it up. Having known both those women, I'll just bet the fur flew. It's a wonder they didn't kill each other.

Kate was working in a house in Wichita that belonged to Jimmy's wife, Bessie. Now Bessie'd been running a cat house in Peoria when Jimmy met her, and she'd followed him to Kansas when the boys got run out of there. If this seems like I'm just going on, it's family history, and it's got to go some place, and learning all this, I didn't have any fears about meeting the old folks when we pulled into their yard. Hell, they knew what their boys was up to, and it didn't make no difference to them. They might've been Methodists, but the way I saw it, they had common sense, too. They was rough as cobs and the salt of the earth, and nothing anybody says will make me change my mind about that.

"Ma! Pa! It's the prodigal son! Git out the fatted calf!" That was Virge, yelling like a Comanche as we pulled in.

He jumped down, helped me down, and left the team standing there. He'd trained 'em to stand dead still when he dropped the lines. I can still hear him saying: "That way, if you fall off the damn' wagon, they won't go off and leave you, or run you over like what happened to Tom."

At the sound of him yelling, they all came running out to look over what sort of critter he'd dragged out of the woods. I felt like a whore in church, wondering how the congregation was going to take to me.

And then the old lady opened her arms wide. "Welcome, daughter," she said, looking at me out of those all-seeing blue eyes of hers, those eyes all her sons inherited, and that could put the fear of God into those that needed it.

She was thin as a whip, but I could feel the strength of her. All bone and muscle she was, a woman who'd borne and raised those boys and three daughters, who'd moved house every time Nick took it in his head to go some place else, who'd crossed the mountains to California and come back, and never once said a word about how hard it was. If the Earps was tough, they'd got a heap of it from her, along with those pale blue eyes that looked straight through a person. They was gunfighter's eyes for a fact, but in Ginnie Ann they hid a kindness and a love of everything living, as I soon found out.

A born doctor, she knew her medicines and her herbs, could set a broken bone, stitch up a wound without fainting, and she always had sick or wounded critters around that she was nursing back to health. And as for horses, there was times, I swear, she talked to 'em and they understood. That pretty mare of hers, Dolly, would come when she was called and follow her like a dog. Ginnie Ann set a store by that mare, took her to California, and rode astraddle with her skirts hiked up, just like a man.

I always wished I could ride like her, but I was never any good. Felt like a sparrow stuck up in the air and not able to fly, and Virge there shouting: "Get him going! Kick him hard!"

"Hopeless," I'd tell him when the ground was once again under my feet.

He'd never let me pick on myself, though. "Why, Allie, nobody's hopeless. Least of all you. I think you're damn' near perfect."

Now I ask you, what woman wouldn't love a man that talked like that? Virge had the gift of it. Morg, too. Tongues like honey, both of 'em. Wyatt not so much, mostly 'cause he wasn't one for fooling and fun. Seems to me he was always thinking about something else, but he sure was a woman-killer when he set his mind to it.

But there I go again, losing my story just because all those folks came crowding into my head so real it seems like last week. Kate said it, though. Too much remembering brings a pain with it that never leaves. She was a wise woman. Brave, too, bless her.

Anyhow, around the corner of the house came Father Earp, who I started calling Grandpa like the kids, and Newton, and behind them a big, strapping girl grinning at me like a cat. That was Adelia, Virge's sister, and we took to each other right off. Funny how that happens. How one look, and you've never been strangers, always been friends.

She said—"It's about time Virge brought me a baby sister!"—and we all broke up, laughing.

I was some years older, but seeing the two of us together, and we was always together, me not quite reaching to her shoulder, you'd have believed what she said. To us, though, it made no difference. We was both young and two of a kind, and over the years that feeling of friendship never changed.

Adelia was engaged to a neighbor boy, Bill Edwards, and all the time we was packing to leave she was watching Virge and me, curious about what being married was all about.

"I love Bill," she said one day. We was taking a walk down near the creek, and the evening was warm and still like a big storm was brewing. "But what's bein' married like?"

I bent down to pull me a stem of grass. "It's happy, long as you love each other." I was thinking of Mattie, pouring herself dry over Wyatt.

Adelia read my mind, being one of those who had the

gift of seeing, not only folks but the future. "You mean like Mattie."

I nodded.

"She and Wyatt ain't married."

"As good as. Or maybe not so good. I sure can't say she's happy."

"You and Virge're different. So are Ma and Pa. And Newton and Jennie. But sometimes I get scared that it won't be like that for Bill and me."

Bill was a nice fella and a hard worker, and like Ma Earp he had a knack with animals. "For sure, you ain't Mattie," I said. "But if you got doubts, better think now."

She stopped and looked toward where the sun was going down in a bank of purple clouds. "No doubts. Just questions I can't ask Ma. And now we're goin' back to California, and I always thought I'd stay right here. Raise a family and put down roots. It's all kind of scary. Like life's changin' too quick."

I'd been scared of change, too. But that was another life. "As long as you and Bill pull together, there's no need to worry," I told her. "Life changes day to day. Look at me and Virge. Married a couple years and already we lived three different places. Where you're livin' ain't as important as who you're livin' with, Deelie, and that's a fact."

She gave a giggle that reminded me of how young she was. "I sure don't want to live in a wagon with Ma and Pa and Bill all the way to California."

"You can share with me and Virge. We won't pay no attention to your fun if you don't mind us, neither."

That said, we went back to the house, giddy as girls.

And when we all pulled out and headed for California, Virge and me, Adelia and Bill was in a wagon together just like I promised.

Chapter Nineteen

So I'd got my wish. To be rolling across the plains in a house on wheels, headed West. It took us a while to get the wagons and teams, stock supplies, pick a route. Grandpa Earp argued for the northern route he'd taken before, but Virge had his eye set on the Santa Fé Trail 'cause he wanted to look over Arizona.

"Besides, I'd just as soon not go through Mormon country again," he said. "I keep thinkin' about Mountain Meadows. Some of those folks are crazy as bedbugs. Look at old Brigham Young."

Grandpa Earp snorted. "That was years ago. Things is different now. Besides, I met Brigham. Got a good head on his shoulders."

Virge sat himself up square in the chair. "You do what you want, but Allie and me's goin' the southern route."

The old man looked like he wasn't used to having a son of his talk back, and like he'd like to whup Virge, but Grandma rapped her knuckles hard on the table.

"I never did trust them Mormons," she said. "They can call it religion, but havin' a bunch of wives sounds like something thought up by a bunch of sinful old men to me, and callin' it religion don't make it right." She gave Grandpa a grin.

He snickered. "Reckon you're right there, Mother. And I reckon we'd all best stick together. No tellin' what troubles we'll meet up with once we get west of Dodge."

She took a big puff on her pipe—always had one going. "We'll make out like always, Mister Earp. We'll make out."

And I believed her, 'cause when that woman made up her mind, the whole world came to heel. Me—all I wanted was to be going, watching the land unfold right before my eyes.

Adelia and Bill got married just before we left, had two nights in a real house on a real bed, and a shivaree neither of 'em ever forgot. We was all happy and excited, and stood outside singing and banging on pots and pans, and calling encouragement to those poor kids till, as Adelia said later, Bill had a mind to pepper us with birdshot.

We pulled out just as the sun came up, and I was as excited as Newton's and Jennie's kids who were whooping and hollering and jumping up and down. I couldn't hardly sit still as the wagons moved into line.

Grandma and Grandpa and Warren Earp was in the first wagon, and Virge and me and Adelia and Bill behind them. Then there was Newton and Jennie, and a wagon with some Cooksey relatives of Grandma's, then a couple more wagons with folks who'd wanted to join up, there being safety traveling together. Behind all that came the stock—extra horses, Grandma's Dolly, and some cows. Warren had a fast horse and did the herding, but Grandpa Earp put a bell on an ox and led it behind his wagon. All the stock, even the horses, learned to follow that ox, and it made it easier to put 'em out to graze. And then there was old Joe, bouncing around like he was on springs, knowing he was going some place far, and far was fine with him.

To my mind we looked every bit as fine as the wagons that had rolled through Ponca Bottom, and I sat there alongside Virge, wrapping my arms around my middle to keep the happiness from busting right out of my skin. We followed the Arkansas River toward Dodge, another town that had sprung up overnight on account of the Texas cattle drives and the railroad pushing West.

Grandma Earp wanted to say good bye to Wyatt, and maybe talk him into coming along, and I was looking forward to seeing Mattie because who knew if we'd see each other again in this life? I needn't have worried about that as it turned out, but, like I said, I never was a fortune-teller, and the present has always been more important to me than what may or may not come next.

It was still too early for the big herds coming from Texas, but there was several thousand longhorns that'd wintered over outside town. I could hear 'em long before they came into sight, and smell 'em, too, and, once we got closer, the stink of buffalo hides stacked up and waiting to be shipped was enough to turn my stomach.

I grabbed hold of Virge's arm. "How long we got to stop here?"

"Long enough for Ma to say her piece to Wyatt. Why?"

" 'Cause without breathin', I won't last."

He chuckled. "I'll see if we can't camp upwind."

We found a place across the river where those cattle hadn't eaten the grass to the ground, but even being upwind didn't help much. And then it started raining, and it was like living in a swamp where the mud stank to heaven.

The men went right off to town, leaving us women back in camp and not happy about it, although Grandma Earp made a real fuss about having to stay home.

Grandpa paid her no mind. "Now, Mother, stop your

fussin'. No sense goin' out and gettin' yourself soaked. Same for you girls. We'll bring Wyatt back with us. Besides, I'd just as soon one of us kept an eye on the stock."

They hadn't been gone half an hour when Dolly whinnied like she always did when strangers came around.

Grandma got up and grabbed her shotgun. "I'm goin' to see what's what."

Outside, it was pouring down rain. She peered out and shook her head. "Can't see a darned thing, but Dolly's as good as a watchdog. Somebody's there."

I came up, holding my own shotgun and wondering where Joe had got to. He always raised a fuss when there was trouble. "I'll go have a look-see," I said. "You stay here and cover me."

Those eyes of hers was blue slits in her face. "You ain't scared?"

"I don't like folks takin' what ain't theirs."

"Then go git 'em. I'll back you."

I climbed down from the wagon and went into the rain.

The horses was milling around in the rope corral, spooked by wind and lightning and by whoever was out there. I spotted him, slipping close to Dolly, who wasn't about to put up with him and shot off into the herd. The man must've figured that with the men gone he could just walk in and take his pick, but what he didn't figure on was Grandma and me, both of us good shots.

"You hold it right there!" I yelled, aiming square at his middle.

He wasn't no fool. Raised his hands and stood facing me. "I'm just lookin' for my horse."

"Your horse ain't here."

He started toward me, coming through the rain that was falling straight down like a curtain. Somewhere a dog was barking. It sounded like Joe, and I figured he'd followed the men to town.

"Don't try nothing," I warned him, and just as I said it a bolt of lightning came so close it shook the ground and spooked the horses good.

The son-of-a-bitch took advantage and run off, but I fired a shot after him, then circled around, trying to get off another.

"Allie!" Grandma and Adelia was hollering.

"I'm here."

"You git him?"

"Hard to tell. I hope I loaded his britches."

Grandma snickered. "Maybe he loaded his own."

Old Joe barked again, closer this time, and then I heard the men all yelling at once.

"You all right?"

"What's that shootin'?"

Virge came out of the rain mad enough to kill and grabbed hold of me. "What in hell're you doin' out here?"

When I told them, Grandpa started cussing. It was Wyatt who stayed calm. "Did you get a look at him, Allie?"

I shook my head. "Not clear. He kept his hat pulled down. But he was tall. Tall as you. And had a black beard."

"That fits about half the men in town," he said. "And this rain's wiped out any tracks. Best set a watch on the stock, day and night. Dutch Henry's been workin' around here lately, too."

Grandma had got back in her wagon. "Ain't you got enough sense to git in out of the rain?" she called. "Come inside and do your talkin' before Allie catches her death."

I didn't, of course. And we never did find out who that stranger was. But you can bet that from that day there was always somebody watching the stock, taking no chances.

The West was full of horse thieves in those days. Likely it still is.

In the morning the sun was out, and the prairie looked like it was covered in little pieces of sparkling glass. The larks was singing, too, flying straight up, then coming down again, all wings and music.

That afternoon, Mattie and Wyatt came out to camp, Wyatt driving a buggy pulled by a fast-stepping horse. It was plain they weren't getting along. He acted like she wasn't there, spent all his time with his pa and Virge, and she sat and pouted till I wanted to shake her.

"Damn it, girl! Where's your pride?" I said, having no patience with temper tantrums.

"I don't have any."

I looked at her hands that wasn't any too clean, and at her red hair that needed a good scrubbing. "A man likes a prideful woman."

"He'll have to like me the way I am."

"Mattie. . . ."

She shushed me. "I don't want to talk about it."

So we sat, not saying a word, and even Grandma Earp who'd come to join us couldn't get more than a yes or a no out of her.

I was damned glad when Wyatt came to where we was sitting and said: "Ready to go?"

She looked up at him, a look so hateful I was shocked to my shoes. Now, I can't say how or why love turns to hate, or even if it's possible, but that afternoon it came home to me that all Mattie's complaining about him not loving her, and how she wasn't a person without him was her twisting the truth. It wasn't love she wanted but to own him, and with a man like Wyatt there was no way in hell she'd get him to do her bidding.

I tell you, she wanted him, body and soul, and whatever she'd felt for him in the beginning was long gone. I guessed he sort of felt responsible for her—getting her involved in horse stealing, then dragging her to Peoria and having her work in Bessie's house, but there wasn't anything more I could see, and I couldn't blame him. It can't feel good to be living with a person who's trying to suck the life out of you every minute, and doesn't give a hoot in hell how she looks while she's doing it.

"Take care of yourself," I said to her, hoping she'd take it as good advice.

She looked at me out of eyes that'd gone flat. "What for?"

There was so many things that came to my mind, I couldn't get a one of 'em out. All I said was—"Damn it, girl, just do it!"—and left her standing there.

Later Grandma came up and said to me: "That girl's got no sense. If she don't want him, why don't she let go?"

"She wants a trained pup."

Those sharp eyes of hers lit up. "She picked the wrong dog. Nobody ever trained Wyatt. Nor any of my boys. Not even me."

Looking back, I doubt anybody ever really did.

Chapter Twenty

I was glad when we rolled out of camp two days later, and never mind that it rained every day and night for a week. It made cooking a chore, but we did as best we could, using dry kindling and the buffalo chips we'd brought along for that purpose. Adelia and I rode in the wagon, playing card games and telling each other stories to pass the time, and just when we couldn't stand being bumped around and shut in any more, the rain quit, and the sun came out, and camp that night was jolly.

The kids was running around playing tag, and after supper an old man who'd joined up with us in Dodge, a man named Bleeker, if I recollect right, got out a mouth organ, and didn't that start our feet tapping! After a bit, Virge picked me up and went two-stepping around till I got dizzy, but Jennie, Newton's wife, said she thought dancing was sinful, and that kind of put an end to the fun.

"Makes you wonder what's not sinful," I grumbled to Virge. "I bet God never said nothin' about folks havin' a good time."

He wiped his face with his big red bandanna. "Methodists don't hold with it. Uncle Renz was against dancin', but he had his fun."

"Yeah," I said. "Dancin's a sin, but crawlin' into bed

with another man's wife is just fine. Seems to me there's something backwards about that."

He didn't answer, and I felt bad for criticizing Renz. "Not that I don't like him anyhow," I added, hoping he'd accept that as an apology.

"Giving up dancin's easy," he said then. "Givin' up the other's askin' too much." He gave me a wink. "For Renz, anyhow."

"Oh, you!" I gave him a push. "It's our night for sleepin' inside, ain't it?"

Since we was sharing the wagon with Adelia and Bill, we switched around—and had caught a big share of teasing for it.

Now, Virge was a man who could pull a solemn face and tell a big windy. Make it so believable I fell for it every time. He looked at me deadpan. "I don't know," he said. "Anyhow, I was thinkin' maybe we oughta give it up. It sort of saps my strength."

Just for a minute I believed him. Just for a minute my world came to an end. And then he laughed.

"~~God~~ damn you, Virge," was all I got out before I was laughing, too. "You oughta be ashamed, puttin' me on like that!"

"And you should've seen your face!"

"Makin' me feel bad."

"Did I?"

"Yeah. You did."

He put his big hands around my face. "That's the last thing I want to do. Ever. Understand?"

For no reason I felt like crying, but choked it back. Funny how a person can go from laughter to tears in the space of a minute, and be wanting nothing more than the comfort of a man's body the next.

"I'm goin' in," I said. "Don't take too long."

After all that rain, the prairie looked like green velvet, miles of it going on and on, and in the hollows, along the creeks, the redbud trees was blooming. I always thought there was something holy about a redbud. Don't know why, but every time I saw one I felt like saying a prayer of thanks, they was that beautiful.

Our party wasn't the only one on the trail. Plenty of folks was on their way West, and the way was plain to see—deep ruts in the green grass, a road cut by wheels and hoofs, and folks like us looking for a better, easier life, or maybe just curious what lay around the next bend, the next rise of the land.

On and on. There was hills, now, and short grass instead of tall. Riding along, you felt the land changing, gathering itself like a live thing, for what, I didn't know. The trees changed, too. The cottonwoods and redbuds was gone, and in their place scraggly cedars, blown crooked by the wind, looking like little old men hunched into themselves.

Although we was always worried about Injuns, we didn't meet any. What trouble we had was from a mustang stud that was running wild and did come in after Dolly. Oh, he was something! Big for a mustang, and black as a raven, and for all Grandma Earp was afraid for her mare, she couldn't help but admire that critter.

"Look at him!" she'd say to whoever was around. "Brave as a lion comin' in this close. Look at the chest on him! He'd make a horse. Oh, yes, he would!" And then: "But he ain't stealin' Dolly. Not long as I'm alive."

Since Dodge, we'd set up a watch on the stock. Had to, 'cause who knew where the next horse thief was coming from out there where we was the law, and make no mistake about that. Out there you took care of your own.

126

Grandma stood her turn, too, and I can still see her setting there in the dark next to Dolly, her shotgun across her knees. "It ain't in me to kill a horse like him," she said more than once. "But I'll sure pepper his rear if he tries something. Maybe teach him a lesson. Or maybe not. No tellin' with the wild ones." He never did come in close, though, and I think she was glad she never had to shoot at him.

Somewhere about then we came up on the biggest herd of buffalo most of us had ever seen, even bigger than the one in the Black Hills. They just covered the plain like a slow-moving black river.

Virge repeated what he'd said to me on the way to Deadwood. "That's got to be the last of 'em. They're goin' fast."

I watched them, and I watched him, wondering what he was thinking. When Virge got hold of an idea, he liked to think it out, beginning to end, and sometimes it took him a while.

"Seems a shame, killin' 'em off," I said. "They was here first. They belong here."

"They're in our way," he said slowly. "Them and the Injuns. It's us that belongs here now. There's not room enough for everybody."

"Get on!" I said. "It'd take a hundred years to fill up this place. Maybe more. Where'd you get a notion like that?"

His eyes was far away, like he was dreaming but wide awake. "I don't know. But it's the truth."

Grandpa Earp walked over to where we'd pulled up. "Might as well camp here. We're not gonna get across that valley till they've moved on. And, besides, I've got me the taste for some buffalo hump. How 'bout it, Virge?"

"I'm your man."

Turned out all the men went buffalo hunting, and from

where we watched it looked easy as swatting flies. Hell! There was so many a man couldn't miss hitting one, and it was more like a slaughter than a hunt. I thought back to all the hides and bones stacked up in Dodge, and figured Virge had been onto something, but it took me years before I really understood what he'd seen so clear that day. All those wagons, all those headed West, were like a flood that couldn't be held back or stopped. A flood that busted its banks, and anything that stood in its way was wiped out, left to rot or to die slow. I'd been scared of things changing once, and I should've been scared that day, seeing as I was a part of the flood, but it hadn't come home to me yet. I was young, and life was good, and nothing ever tasted as sweet as fresh-killed buffalo meat.

The wind was blowing from the southwest, hot and dry and coming in gusts that like to've blown my bonnet right off me. That wind blew, and the sun climbed up and never seemed to go down, just sat there, burning everything in sight.

At first I made fun of Virge, whose face was dark as an Injun's except where his hat covered his forehead. "You look like you painted yourself."

He wasn't happy. Taking the Cimarrón Cut-Off had been his idea, and the rest of our party, including Grandpa Earp, was grumbling about how he'd made a mistake and led us into hell.

"If you looked in a mirror, you'd scare yourself," he snapped, then walked away, worry sitting heavy on his shoulders.

I didn't need a mirror to tell me what I looked like—a dried-up insect, good for nothing and ready to blow away. The heat, the wind, the need to ration our water had turned us all into crones, even Adelia. She'd got burned bad, and the skin on her face was coming off in patches. Even the salve Grandma gave her didn't help.

The stock had the worst of it, pulling us day in and day out, with no graze to speak of and only the water we doled out. Old man Bleeker's oxen had gone sore-footed, and he kept falling behind us—so far we once or twice had to send someone back to look for him and wasted time we couldn't spare.

The day came when all the water we had left was nothing but green scum that turned you just looking at it. But it was wet, and that's what counted, and I took my cup, closed my eyes, and drank, hoping it wouldn't come right back up. That's what thirst does to you. Makes you so desperate you'll drink anything, and your throat so dry, your tongue so stiff, you start thinking you might never be able to swallow water if you had it. And all that time Virge was blaming himself for getting us in a pickle.

"Damn it, Allie! It seemed so smart back in Kansas. All those miles saved. But I never figured on this."

I put my hands on his shoulders, felt them bunched up and tight, and tried hard to find something cheerful to say. "Maybe tomorrow we'll come to water. Got to be some somewhere."

"Sure. Just not here."

"Well, dyin's not in the cards. Deelie told fortunes last night."

He gave a snort. "Cards! Games! What good are they when we're dyin'? Did she say where there's any water?"

"Nope."

"Tomorrow, early, I'm going to ride ahead, and I won't be back till I find some."

"Alone?" I hated thinking of him out there and nothing

around but a thousand miles of desert and wind.

"It's best."

"Promise you'll come back."

He turned around, pulled me on his lap, and kissed me. "I'll try my damndest, Allie. I don't want to lose you."

And there was nothing to do but settle for that.

I saw him off just before sunup. He was riding his bay horse, Roman, that was part mustang and tough as rawhide. If any horse would get through, it was Roman. That's all the consolation I had that day as we kept on rolling across that hard, stony ground, with the wind picking up, and dust everywhere, and that sun that never seemed to move. I prayed that day, although I never put much stock in the notion that God would work a miracle just on account of somebody's asking for it. I prayed in my head. My lips was so dry I couldn't have said a word out loud. And just when I was about to quit, just when Grandpa's lead horse stumbled and stopped in its tracks, we heard it. A horse coming at a trot.

"Praise God!" Grandma scrambled off the wagon and went running to meet Virge, looking like a tumbleweed, her skirts blowing, her legs going every which way, and her arms spread wide.

Not three miles from where we stopped was water—a pond of it coming out of nowhere—and green grass all around. There was rejoicing that night. We filled our barrels, filled our bellies, and the stock drank till it seemed they'd empty that puddle. They didn't, though. It just kept filling up on its own, probably from a spring. I didn't know, didn't care. Maybe it was a miracle. I can't say. But we camped there two days, resting the stock and waiting for old man Bleeker to catch up.

We heard his wagon creaking along, and we heard him

singing. It was the strangest thing, that that old man could come so close to dying and still be singing, the music echoing out to nowhere, and him not caring a hoot.

I said to Virge that maybe he'd gone crazy—alone, maybe wanting to end it all by dying.

But Virge shook his head. "He's got more gumption than any ten men. There's nothing crazy about courage."

He was right about that. I've seen enough courage since to recognize it when it hits me.

Chapter Twenty-One

We was on the High Plains now, grand, rolling country, and far away west, like a storm building on the horizon, was the Sangre de Cristo Mountains. When Virge explained to me that meant the Blood of Christ Mountains, I pondered over why anybody'd give them such a name. "Seems a funny thing to call a pile of rocks."

"The Spanish gave funny names to lots of places."

"What Spanish?" You can tell how ignorant I was.

He clucked to the team. "Maybe the Spanish who live here. Or maybe the ones who came first lookin' for gold."

"They find any?"

"Not that I ever heard. Just Injuns and buffalo. And a bit of trouble. But a lot of 'em stayed. Las Vegas, Santa Fé, Albuquerque, they're still mostly Spanish towns."

Well, I kept my eyes on those mountains, no matter what they was called, and each day we got closer to 'em. We'd crossed the Canadian River and was moving down a long, wide valley cut with creeks and filled with antelope—so many that, when they ran, it looked like the whole earth was running.

One night Adelia and I was frying up some of that antelope meat, and I happened to look toward the mountains and saw they was turned blood red. I tell you, I stood and stared, wishing I somehow could get a hold of that color, that picture shining right in front of my eyes.

"Virge!" I called out, and pointed.

He stared at them a minute, and a slow smile spread across his face. "Reckon you got your answer, Allie," was all he said. And I reckoned those old Spanish had thought long and hard, but that they'd got it right, at least the part about the blood.

Las Vegas, the first town we hit after leaving Dodge, was just about up against those mountains and looked out on the end of the High Plains. I'd get up every morning and look east across those plains that ended in a jumble of hills and gullies, covered in grass. And then I'd turn around and face the other way, wondering how anybody ever found their way up and over those peaks, they was so high, so damned immovable, standing there as if daring us to try.

We laid over several weeks in that little town, making repairs to the wagons, and trading with the locals for horses and supplies we'd used up long before. And I have to say I was kind of regretful when we pulled out. Maybe it was just the strangeness of the people, the language that they spoke so softly, or maybe it was that view—rolling hills, the sky spilling out above our heads blue as a jaybird's wing, and those mountains. Since then I've seen and climbed more mountains than I want to count, but they was the first, and the sight of 'em, pushing back the plains and holding up heaven has stuck with me to this day. Just like my first sight of Santa Fé has stuck with me.

It was a little town of mud houses and twisted streets, and everywhere you went you smelled the piñon cooking fires, sweet as the wind off the mountains. That's all you could see looking out—mountains covered with trees, and away south what looked like a yellow carpet spread across a valley, with some black hills and a river making a border. Those little streets was filled with folks going about their business—burros carrying wood, women with shawls wrapped around themselves, traders from everywhere selling whatever they'd come to sell, and children, lots of 'em, dark-haired and giggling, running free as birds. And then there was the Injuns who came to sell their turquoise and their cooking pots, and everyone gabbling away in Spanish or some other lingo I couldn't understand.

Virge bought me a bean pot from one of those Injuns, and I kept it for years, although to tell the truth, that same Injun had a turquoise brooch I wanted so bad I couldn't stand it. Now I never was one for decking myself out fancy, and I never begged for presents, but it was such a pretty thing, all shiny silver around a piece of stone blue as the sky. I stood there and didn't say a word, took the pot in my hands, and walked away without looking back, not once. If I had, I'd have seen Virge slip some money to that Injun and pocket the brooch. He knew without me telling him, see. That's how he was. And next morning, when I got up, there it was, pinned to my old, raggedy dress and shining in a beam of sunlight.

We followed the Río Grande to Albuquerque, and then turned west. Grandpa Earp and Virge was curious to see Arizona. The rest of the train followed along, although to tell the truth hard feelings had sprung up since we'd crossed the Cut-Off. Newton's wife, Jennie, was fussing because she hadn't seen a church for a thousand miles, and she was afraid her children would turn into heathens, or worse yet, Catholics like the Mexicans, and Grandma's Cooksey relatives hadn't expected any such hardship as drinking scum water and nearly dying from the heat and dust, and them "foreigners" as they called the Mexicans they'd had to deal with—and probably got the worst of the dealing for their attitude.

Grandma was right put out at them, and one day just spoke out plain. "If you don't like it, then take yourselves back home. Bellyachin' don't fix what's broke, and the West's no place for sissies."

Of course, they took offense and kept to themselves from then on, like they was too good for the rest of us. Crossing Arizona, things got worse, and by the time we got to Prescott hardly anybody was speaking to anybody else. Virge told me this happened often with folks made to travel together and facing hardships. Sooner or later, tempers got stretched, and fighting started. "That's why we have to have a good wagon boss," he said. "That's why we got to listen to Pa, no matter what we or anybody thinks."

I didn't much care, but at Prescott I'd had a belly full and said so, mostly to Jennie who'd got on my nerves more than once with her grousing about heathens.

"If you miss church-goin' so much, why don't you just go on back? Seems to me God's every place you look, so, if you can't see Him, maybe you're the heathen."

We was camped in the pine woods, mountains all around, and the air so sweet it was like the world was brand new. We'd come through the worst of it, and there she was acting put upon.

She turned on me like her kind always does. "Don't you preach to me, Allie," she said, breathing fire. "If anybody's a heathen, it's you."

"And proud of it!"

"Allie!" That was Virge, calling me over to our wagon.

"What?" I was mad clear through.

"Don't get in a hair-pullin' match. It won't do no good.

What would you say if I said I'm of a mind to stay here for a bit?"

"Here? You mean not go to California?"

He nodded. "There's some that want to turn back. Newt and Jennie and the Cookseys. They're not cut out for it, and that's fine with me, but Pa's dead set on gettin' to California."

"And you ain't?"

"I'm down to our last dollar. It wouldn't hurt to stop a while. Find a job, earn some money."

I thought about the brooch he'd bought, probably spending what we could have used for something practical, and looked around me, feeling bad inside. The sky was so blue it hurt my eyes, and a big white cloud was pushing up behind the mountains. It struck me that I was happy just being alive and with Virge, and where we were didn't matter so much as that we were together, and I put the brooch and the money spent on it out of my head.

"Is Deelie and Bill stayin'?" I asked.

"They're goin' on."

I knew I'd miss her, but folks did what they had to do, and a friendship like she and I had wouldn't break because we was apart. Besides, what I had with Virge was stronger than whatever was between Adelia and me.

So I said: "Then it's just us. And about time. And I reckon California ain't goin' nowhere anytime soon."

For that I got a hug that damned near squeezed the breath out of me, and that's how we ended up staying in Prescott for nearly two years.

We sold our wagon and found a cabin, but we needed a corral for the horses and went right to work on that. Virge was doing a little law work, and had taken a timber claim—there was always a need for wood in those days and money to be made cutting and hauling it—and he brought in the rails. I took some money from the sale of the wagon and bought calico to make curtains.

Matter of fact, I was just climbing on a chair to hang 'em when two men on horseback went by. They was running flat out, which I thought was damned foolish in a country where a horse could break a leg just putting a foot down wrong. It wasn't but a few minutes later that the sheriff and a couple men came along, driving a buckboard, and hollered for Virge. He went to see what the fuss was about, then came running to the house and grabbed his rifle.

"What's goin' on? Who're those men? Where you goin?" I was hopping up and down.

"Those two were shooting up the town. We're going after them. You stay in the house, you hear?"

"And you be careful!" I shouted after him, but I should've saved my breath. Careful wasn't a word that meant anything to any of the Earps. When it came to a pinch, they just went in fighting.

When the shooting started, I could hear it plain—and the echoes that made it seem like all one, long sound—and all I could think of was Virge out there getting shot at, maybe killed. Never mind he'd told me to stay in the house. I went running toward that sound, calling his name.

"Virge! Virge!" The cañon caught that, too, and threw it back at me so it was like there was two of me shouting.

And then Virge stepped out of the brush and caught me, picked me straight up in the air, my feet still moving. "Whoa," he said. "Where d'you think you're going?"

"To make sure you ain't dead!"

His laugh boomed out just like always. "Why, honey, it'd take more than two drunk saddlebums to get me. And next time I tell you to stay in the house, you do it. I can't afford to lose you."

"You don't know what it's like sittin' there, waitin'!" I was fighting off tears.

He set me down easy. "I reckon I don't."

And I reckon he spoke the truth. It's us women who sit at home, worrying, jumping at every noise, sick at heart because come to it there ain't a thing we can do once the fighting starts.

The buckboard came up the trail. In it was a dead man and another, bad hurt and looking like he might puke. I hoped he did. Hoped he choked on it for scaring me and who knows who else out of our wits and putting Virge in danger. It's a good thing I couldn't know what lay ahead for us. As it is, I'm sorry we ever left Prescott, sorry I ever heard the name of that hell hole they named Tombstone.

Chapter Twenty-Two

It was Virge who heard about the silver strike in Tombstone. He came home one night carrying a newspaper and said: "Allie, I been thinkin'."

And I said: "Then quit. Every time you try, you get us in trouble." I was teasing, of course, but he didn't laugh, just went on like he hadn't heard.

"We never planned to stay here this long. There's money to be made other places. Look how we made out in Deadwood. Right now I feel like I'm just standin' still, and I'm not made right for that. With this silver strike I could be freightin', haulin' in what's needed, and there's always things needed in any new place. And"—he gave a grin—"money to be made at the tables."

I looked at our little cabin in the trees. It was home. Warm in winter, cool in summer when I left the door open and the wind came through. "You set on this?" I asked after a bit.

He tugged on his mustache. "I'm thinkin' on it, like I said. Maybe I'll write Wyatt. I bet he's had a belly full of Dodge and Texas cowboys by now, knowin' him. If we threw in together, we could make a go of it. Maybe run a stage line."

"Where'd you say this place was?"

"South of here. They call it Tombstone."

I've said over and over that I can't see the future, but when he said that, a chill grabbed me deep in my bones. "I hope it ain't ours."

"You tryin' to scare me off?"

"Just sayin' what I feel. It don't sound exactly like a friendly place. Who named it that, anyhow?"

"You said the same thing about the mountains in New Mexico," he reminded me. "There's no accounting for names. Your ma called you Alvira, and you don't like that, either."

"It don't feel like me."

He was standing in the door, the light streaming in from behind him so his face was in shadow, but even so I caught the look in his eye and stood stockstill, waiting for what I knew was coming.

"You always feel just right." He tossed down the paper and held his arms out, and in spite of my worries I walked into them.

With my face against his chest I said—"Is this how you're gettin' around me?"—and heard his big laugh coming up from his belly.

"Yeah," he said, "and I can't think of a better way to do it."

Well, Virge sent off his letter, and it wasn't any time at all before Wyatt, Mattie, Bessie and Jim, and Bessie's two kids got to Prescott. They came in two big Concord coaches with a herd of horses trailing behind, and I figured Wyatt must've been helping himself to good stock all the way from Dodge.

"So. We're all together again." The voice came from behind me, but there was no mistaking it. Sure enough, there was Kate and Doc, too, both of 'em grinning.

"Where'd you come from?" I gave Kate a hug.

"Las Vegas. Doc was taking the cure."

"If that's what you want to call it," Doc said. "The cure was worse than the damned bug."

She gave him one of her disgusted looks. "And you should have stayed. But, no. Wyatt calls, and you come running."

He didn't answer, but he looked a lot better than he had in Deadwood. Maybe he had a few years left. I hoped so for Kate's sake. She wasn't looking so good herself, but I didn't have time to say anything because Virge came up with two folks I hadn't met and leading two children by their hands.

"This here's Bessie," he said. "And her kids, Frank and Hattie. And this skinny old coot's my big brother Jim. Meet my bride."

"I'll be god damned." Jim grabbed my hand and pumped it up and down. "You're little enough you could hide in the son-of-a-bitch's damned pocket." Then he threw back his head and laughed.

Bessie said: "Don't mind him. He just can't talk without cussing."

I was laughing, too. By then I'd gotten used to everybody making a smart remark about my size, had almost came to expect it. Besides, among themselves the Earps was jolly, always poking fun at each other, at least early on.

When Virge stopped laughing, he said: "Methodism didn't take on Jimmy no matter how hard Ma tried."

By then I was in the spirit of the reunion. "Well, hell," I said, "I always admired good cussin'." And that set us off again.

But we didn't laugh much longer. I took the women, and Bessie's two kids, Frank and Hattie, inside, and the men went off to tend the stock, and that's when Kate turned white as a frog belly and let out a sound that damned near froze me in my tracks.

Bessie caught her just before she fell, and together we got her onto the bed. It didn't take us long to find out she was losing a child, and less time than that to see her heart was breaking.

"I wanted it so badly." Her whisper was so low, she sounded like she was talking to herself. "I hoped we could be a real family."

"Ridin' in that coach all the way here sure didn't help," I said. "But you can try again."

She kept on like she hadn't heard. "Doc and Wyatt. Doc and Wyatt. It's always Wyatt, never me. Why can't he let us alone? Why can't we be like other people?"

I took a rag and wiped her face. Her hair had come out of its bun. She had pretty hair, pale gold and lots of it, and it was stuck to her cheeks with sweat and tears. I don't know how I knew enough to answer the way I did, but I said: "Because you ain't like other people. Maybe none of us is."

She looked straight at me out of those blue eyes. I saw her unhappiness was gone, and she was mad clear through. "Gypsies," she hissed through her teeth. "We're all a bunch of damned Gypsies. I want to go home."

"Where's home?" I asked, feeling bad for her.

She shut her eyes. "No place. That's the trouble. Just like a Gypsy. Now go away and leave me alone."

Bessie and I had got the bleeding stopped, so I did like she wanted. Outside, I found Mattie sitting on the little porch, looking like a rag doll somebody had thrown out.

"Don't tell me you're breedin', too," I said.

Her mouth twisted. "Not hardly. I have a headache from ridin' in that damned thing."

"I've got a powder if you want it."

"I've got my own."

That's when I noticed her eyes. Although I didn't know then what laudanum does, I recognized trouble when I saw it. "Don't take any more."

"And don't tell me what to do. Everybody's always tryin' to tell me that. Like I don't have a mind of my own."

Bessie had gone to find Doc, and I saw them coming back across the yard.

Now, you can say what you want about Doc Holliday, but he was as shocked and as miserable as Kate was. "How is she?" he asked me. "She won't . . . she's not going to . . . ?" He couldn't get out the word.

"She ain't dyin'," I told him. "She wanted to be alone a while, but you go on in. She needs you."

He shook his head. "She doesn't need anybody. She just thinks she does." But he stepped up on the porch and went through the door.

I pulled Bessie to one side. "What's Mattie takin'?"

She shook her head. "Anything she can get. I can't stop her."

"How about Wyatt?"

She snorted. "I don't think he gives a damn one way or the other, and I'm not sure I can blame him."

I stood there in the bright sunlight, the horses nickering in the corral, the voices of the men and kids coming from what seemed like far away, and the cares of the world, the hurting, the pain folks give to each other came down and sat on my shoulders heavy as stone.

For a minute I wished I was a kid again, running barefoot along the creek, with the only thing in my head the magic of water moving over stones, the birds making music in the air. For a minute I wished Virge hadn't got a bee in his bonnet about going to Tombstone, and that it was just the two of us sitting down to supper like always, with old Joe begging hand-outs under the table, and the lamp shining on our faces, and out in the pines an owl hooting.

As it was, I had my work cut out for me that night and all the rest of the time it took for us to pack up. Our house was so full of folks coming and going that I never had a chance to take a breath, didn't hardly have time to grieve over leaving home another time.

Wyatt had already got himself a job as shotgun guard for Wells Fargo. He'd met a fella, Jim Hume in Las Vegas, and got hired on the spot. Off and on he'd worked for Wells Fargo over the years, so he wasn't with us when we finally pulled out.

But I'll say one thing. He'd stood up for me when it came to taking my sewing machine to Tombstone. I set a store by that machine, one of the first things Virge'd bought me when we got a little money, and leaving it behind felt to me like leaving part of my body.

I was standing in the yard trying to figure how to fit it in with the rest of the stuff and was near to crying, especially since Virge had told me there wasn't room.

Wyatt came by and took one look at me—I must've been a sight—and said: "Take the damn' thing. Moving's bad enough without making the women miserable."

"You mean it?" I was surprised, because Wyatt didn't generally pay attention to things like that.

He gave me a look out of those pale blue eyes of his. "I don't say what I don't mean, Allie. We'll toss out something or other, but you can have your sewing machine."

And that's how, when we pulled out of Prescott, that machine rode with us all the way to Tombstone where, at the end, it got left anyhow.

Virge had got himself a job, too. Crawley Dake, the U.S. marshal for Arizona Territory, had got to know Virge after the shooting of the two hardcases. When he got wind of us going to Tombstone, he appointed Virge deputy U.S. marshal for the district.

"You know what that means." Virge was shining his fancy new badge on his pant leg.

"What?"

"Means I'm the law and you got to do what I tell you."

"And if I don't?"

"I'll throw you in jail. Let you loose on the prisoners."

Of course, he was teasing, but I could do that, too. "And maybe I'd get some peace and quiet for a change, instead of having to listen to you and your brothers jabber all the time."

"Jabber? Jabber? Us?" He was laughing so hard his eyes was almost shut.

"Yeah, you. But at least nobody's turned the table over and broke my dishes yet."

"Just you wait," he said, and grabbed my hands, pulling me close.

"I'd rather not. And I'm proud of you, although maybe it don't seem like it. Virge Earp, U.S. marshal. Sounds good to me."

"Sounds as good as you feel."

"If you're thinkin' what I'm thinkin'," I said, "we'd better go out back. This place is like an ant hill. Anybody's likely to walk in."

"There's no law against it," he reminded me, still laughing. "And I *am* the law now."

"That badge didn't give you much sense." I pulled him out the door, wondering how long it'd be before we were alone again. As it turned out, it was a mighty long time.

Chapter Twenty-Three

The women and kids was all crammed into one of the coaches. The other was full of our belongings, including my sewing machine tied on behind. I looked out at our little house as we drove off, and there must've been tears in my eyes because Bessie reached over and patted my hand.

"It's hard leavin' a place you love. Lord knows, I've done it before, and it never gets any easier. But at least you've got Virge and I've got Jim. It'd be worse without them."

I sneaked a look at Mattie who seemed to be sleeping, and just as well, because she was more like an orphan being dragged from place to place than Wyatt's wife or even his woman. Bessie caught my look and shook her head in agreement.

"How'd you meet Jim?" I asked her then, nosey as usual.

She had pretty, blue-gray eyes, and, when she smiled, they lit up like the sun was in them. "He came in where I was working. We took one look at each other and . . . well, here we are."

"Whyn't you tell her where you was workin'?" Mattie sat up in her corner, blinking.

"It's no secret. I did what I had to do to keep food on the table. I was a widow with two kids and no husband, so let the world think what it wants."

Bessie didn't get mad often, but I could tell she was thinking about it.

She went on, and her voice was cold: "I took you in when you got to Peoria, and you were glad of it. And I paid your fines when you got arrested for your damn' fool tricks, so don't make keepin' a house sound shameful. It isn't. It's a business like any other, and a darn' good one. It kept you from starving, miss, and don't you forget it."

Mattie sniffed, like she was going to cry. "I didn't mean. . . ."

"I know you didn't. Your problem is you always talk before you think, and then you get mad at everybody. We're all stuck in this coach until we get where we're goin', so try and be nice."

For once Mattie didn't answer back. She just curled up in her corner and shut her eyes. Leave it to her, though, to get everybody riled and sticking pins in each other. I wondered if she'd always been like that, or if she was just plain unhappy and couldn't help herself. Still, I decided I'd ignore her.

"I got nothin' against runnin' a house," I said to Bessie. "If it wasn't for the one in Omaha, I might've starved."

Mattie opened her eyes. "So you ain't any better than the rest of us."

It was my turn to get mad, and I did. "I was the washwoman, and you know it. And if you're goin' to sit there snipin' at us, I'm ridin' up top with Virge just to be shut of you."

"Me, too!" Both kids hollered at the same time. "We want to ride with Uncle Virge and Uncle Jim, too!"

Bessie gave them a look. "You do your lessons like I said. Uncle Virge don't want to be bothered keeping an eye on a pair of monkeys. Jim, neither."

Hattie giggled. "I'm not either a monkey."

"You'll do till one comes along."

We got quiet after that. Bessie and I looking out the windows and hoping we'd get to Tombstone quick.

We drove on south through Phoenix and Tucson that back then was just little towns full of mud houses and not much else, though there was an Army fort at Tucson mainly on account of the Apaches who'd been making trouble in those parts for a long time.

Wyatt met us in Tucson and told us we weren't gonna be able to do what the boys had planned—open a stage line—'cause there already were two lines into Tombstone and no room for a third. That was a real shame, since they all was good teamsters, even Jim, who had to pretend his shoulder was crippled to get his Civil War pension. Hell, he was driving a hack in San Bernardino when he was an old man!

We sold our coaches and a lot of the horses, kept our riding horses and two heavy teams, and bought two wagons and had canvas tops made for 'em. And that's the way we went into Tombstone in early December.

Now there's some who call that country a desert, but it ain't. The Injuns loved the place so much they fought and died for it, and they had reason—all those long valleys with mountains in between and little rivers running through, and in the December light everything shining and sharp-edged against a sky blue as turquoise. There was even something blooming although the nights was cold. We had a big camp-fire every night and slept in the wagons under lots of blankets, but, before I turned in, I always took a minute to look up at the stars—so many nobody could've counted 'em, or named 'em all.

We came down to the San Pedro River at a place called

Contention that had a smelter, and from there it was a good pull uphill to Tombstone. You could smell the place from far off—wood smoke, dust, animals, and horses, mostly them, and people, all jammed together in tents, shacks, whatever came to hand. It's a funny thing how a town can grow where there was nothing but rocks and scrub a few years before. How a gold nugget or a chunk of silver can make fools or killers out of men who was never either one before the bug bit 'em. Or maybe we're all a little bit of both, come to think.

But we drove in filled with high hopes. We was all young and healthy, and even Mattie seemed to perk up at the prospect of a new place and maybe a new start. Little did she know. It was the beginning of the end for her. In fact, it was the beginning of a curse put on the whole bunch of us. If the Earp boys hadn't been fighters, none of it would have happened, but they never backed off from what had to be done. Virge went in there as a lawman, and Wyatt was working for Wells Fargo, and it was only natural they'd lock horns with the scum that had already collected there like buzzards. There was cattle thieves, stagecoach hold-up men, and killers, all looking to make out. Most of 'em had been run out of Texas and New Mexico and figured they'd found paradise in southeast Arizona. But it's a place I came to hate and still do. I wouldn't go back there so much as a day, and I'm sorry we ever went at all. Just like Sadie kept saying: "Evil come up out of the ground."

For a long time, though, life was pleasant. We camped out and lived in tents and in the wagons till we found us some lots and built our houses. Virge and me built on the southwest corner of Frémont Street, and Wyatt and Mattie built one just to the west of us with a lot in between. Wyatt built a shed for his horses in the back, saying he wasn't gonna trust them to no livery stable. He set a store by his racing horse, Dick Naylor, a big stud, and never a day passed that he didn't spend time with that horse, just another habit that irritated Mattie and put her in a sulk.

"He pays more attention to that critter than he does to me," she said once, and I didn't tell her that the horse nickered and came running when he laid eyes on Wyatt, which was more than she did.

Jim's and Bessie's place was on the northeast corner of the same street, and, if I wanted company, all I had to do was open the door and holler, and Bessie the same. We women stuck together, did our washing in my yard, and hung it out, and most often, in the evenings when the boys was out gambling, we'd sit around my parlor mending socks and shirts, or sewing curtains to put up at our windows, and just having ourselves a good gossip about the way things were going.

For those few months, it seemed like we had the world in our pockets. We had money, we had roofs over our heads, and we had the time to enjoy ourselves, even though the boys was often busy searching out water rights and mineral claims. But they often took us with them in the light delivery wagon that belonged to Wyatt, and that he liked to use in case he camped out a night or two.

Virge would say—"How about us havin' a picnic tomorrow?"—and he never got no for an answer.

When spring comes to the San Pedro Valley, it's like no place else. The cottonwoods down by the river are the first to show little, green leaves, then the mesquites follow and start in blooming along with everything else. I remember one day in particular. The boys was looking for water and springs over by the Huachuca Mountains, hoping to file water rights, and us women went along for the ride. We'd packed a picnic and was as excited as Hattie and Frank at being out and seeing things. That was the first time I ever saw the poppies blooming—enough of 'em that it seemed the hills and slopes was on fire. Must have been a million of 'em—yellow and pale orange—all blowing in the breeze till I got dizzy just looking.

Wouldn't you know that Virge pulled up the wagon, jumped out, and started picking till he couldn't hold 'em all. "For the Earp ladies, God bless 'em," he said, handing 'em over. Our laps was filled with the little things, their petals so soft, so shiny it was a shame to touch them 'cause they withered so quick. But Bessie started weaving a chain, like we used to make out of daisies, and before long we was all wearing necklaces of yellow poppies. Virge was singing some song at the top of his lungs, the kids was singing along, and Bessie was laughing.

"We must look like a travelin' circus," she said.

"Except there's nobody here to see us."

Mattie gave a sniff. "Just as well. We look like damn' fools, if you ask me."

Oh, she could try your patience! To tell the truth, I kept my thoughts to myself, but I always wondered how in hell Wyatt put up with her for so long. Maybe he felt guilty on account of the horse stealing, or maybe at one time he felt something stronger for her, but when the end came, and it did, he was more than ready to leave her.

"Now for the ladies' high-wire act!" Virge yelled, pullin' up the team alongside a wash that was running just a trickle but with enough water for the horses and some shade from a big cottonwood tree for us. "Step right up, folks, and see Miz Bessie somersault through the air."

She snickered. "In a pig's ass."

I thought she was getting to cuss better every day due to

being around Jim, and liked her the better for it.

"You behave," I said to Virge, and he said: "Make me."

"Not in front of the kids."

"Next time, we're comin' alone. How'd you like that?"

"I'd like it fine."

We never did make it out there by ourselves, but I got that afternoon stuck in my mind and can't ever forget it—that sky blue and without a cloud to disturb it, the way the valley opened up as it ran south, so it looked like it went on forever, and looking down on us, those mountains, dark and rough like something out of a fairy tale, a place you wouldn't want to get lost in and mightn't get out of if you did.

There was other days, though, like the time Virge and me went down to the river to pick us some cottonwood switches for our yard. I'd been complaining about the fact that there wasn't any shade, and that when the wind blew it like to picked me up and carried me away. Besides that, I figured the trees might stop some of the dust that was always blowing in, especially in the spring when the wind never stopped blowing. I swear, I swept dirt out the back, and it circled around and came in the front, and keeping house was a chore.

The San Pedro's a nice river, but it's sure not the Missouri or the Cimarrón, more like what back in Nebraska we called a creek. Still, it was pretty down there, the water running over stones, doves calling in the brush, and the mesquites so thick in places a person had to fight to get through the tangle. And the thorns! Those mesquites, some of 'em, had thorns two inches long!

We walked a bit, Virge carrying a shovel and a burlap sack, and me investigating every switch and young tree I passed. I wanted them all—wanted a forest around that house, probably because I'd got used to living with trees all around. It took me so long making up my mind that Virge got impatient.

"Lord's sake, Allie, a tree's a tree. Take your pick and let's get goin'."

"You got something better to do?"

That kind of stopped him. He leaned on the shovel. "Nope."

"Well, then, let's enjoy ourselves. Just us for a change." It seemed like back in town there was always somebody around or underfoot, and I hadn't realized till right then how I missed being alone with my husband.

"Is my family gettin' to you?" he wanted to know.

I shook my head. "It's just nice bein' by ourselves in the quiet. Talkin' without somebody bustin' in and wantin' something."

Those eyes of his that could scare a man to death but never scared me once started twinkling. "Is that all?"

I looked around. Saw water, trees, a covey of quail running for cover, and the little, sandy place where I was standing. "Put down that shovel," I said. "We can talk later."

There's an ache in me still just thinking about that day. I'll never be done missing that man. Sure, he was a hard man, and tough, and he killed those that needed killing like any good lawman did then and now, but when we was together, he was somebody else, somebody only I ever saw, full of fun and laughter and caring.

The sun was over the Huachucas, and there was shadows laying on the water when I looked again. "The day got away from us."

"Naw. It's ours to keep."

He was right, and I kept it inside for sixty years, just like

I kept the thought of those two cottonwoods we finally dug out and took home. "You'll spend your life waterin' them," he warned me, and it was a chore keeping 'em alive. In those early days Tombstone had no water except what the men hauled in by wagon or in bags on little burros. Later there was a pipeline laid from the Huachucas—out of Sheffield steel, so they said—but not then.

Still, I did my best, saved the wash water and cared for those trees like they was babies that me and Virge had made that afternoon. And I got my reward when they shot up, branched out, and made me purely light-headed just having them there.

Chapter Twenty-Four

It wasn't till the next summer that the trouble started. Virge was serving law papers and that sort of thing, and bringing in a little money, but the buzzards hadn't yet collected to feast on the place. The reason I can make sense out of the tangle that happened, remembering names and dates and such, is that when I decided to tell my story like it really was, I asked LaVonne Miller, Adelia's granddaughter, to help me. We started with my copy of that writer's story, and he at least got the names right, although when LaVonne read what he'd written, I thought she'd have a hissy fit.

She showed it to her mother, Adelia's daughter, Estelle, and her father Bill got hold of it. Well, he was madder than me, said he'd like to strangle the bastard. He might yet. Killing is in Bill's blood. His pa killed more men than all the Earp boys put together, although he's just as nice a fella as you'd ever want to meet. So is Bill.

Other writers wrote about the Earps and Tombstone. There was that man Burns, who went to Wyatt before he died and said he wanted to do his story. When Wyatt told him that John Flood, his close friend, had already written it, Burns asked Wyatt to help him do a book on Doc Holliday. That was just an excuse to get Wyatt talking, 'cause when the book came out, it was about the Earps and not Doc. If Wyatt hadn't been old and sick, he'd have looked Burns up and sieved the bastard, and who'd have blamed him? I can remember how mad he and Sadie was— her especially, 'cause she thought they should've got a cut of the money.

Seems like everybody's trying to make money off what happened. There was that Lake fella, too, but he waited till Wyatt was dead, and he got some of it right, and Sadie got a little money. Not enough, though. There's not enough money in the world to make up for what happened in Tombstone. My stomach still hurts when I get to thinking about it.

The first trouble we had with the crooks that was gathering around came when Billy Clanton stole Wyatt's horse. I can remember Wyatt busting in, breathing fire, and saying: "Some son-of-a-bitch stole Dick Naylor."

"Where the hell was he?" Virge wanted to know.

"Like a damn' fool I left him hobbled out so he could eat a little grass. He was in the empty lot behind the stable. I'll find out who did it, though."

Virge shook his head. "I wouldn't be too sure about that."

"You can bet on it!"

By then, Wyatt had a bunch of snitches put together, probably paying 'em with Wells Fargo money, so he had a handle on what was going on. It took a couple days, but he came in and said: "The bastard's down in Charleston. I'm goin' after him."

"Want company?" Virge was already on his feet.

"No need."

Well, when he got down there, damn if he didn't see Billy Clanton riding Dick Naylor down the street bold as brass. He followed him, and, when Billy hitched the horse in front of a saloon, Wyatt walked up and said: "I'll take my horse back now."

I have to laugh, picturing that, 'cause I can just see how Wyatt looked saying it. Most men would've stopped right there, but Billy, being a dumb cowboy, put up a fuss, and Wyatt drew on him.

"Why didn't you run him in?" Virge wanted to know.

"Too damn' much trouble. He'd have been out in a day or two, anyhow. But when he found out I was letting him off, the little son-of-a-bitch had the nerve to ask for his saddle back."

"And?" Knowing his brother, Virge was already chuckling.

"And nothing. I took it off outside of town and threw it in a ditch. Rode home bareback. I'm keepin' the bridle. It's silver-mounted."

"I reckon he won't come lookin' for it."

"If he does, he'll get more than he asked for. And I'm lockin' the stable door."

"About time," I put in. "And who's this Clanton fella, anyhow?"

Wyatt gave me a look that said I was butting in where I shouldn't, but said: "There's a bunch of 'em over in the Animas Valley. An old man and a bunch of sons. Cow rustlers. None of 'em any damn' good."

It turned out that Billy, his brother Ike, and the old man was the heads of the gang that was gathering around Tombstone, and the McLowery boys threw in with 'em. And then Curly Bill got together the biggest gang of outlaws in the West.

A little while later, Charlie Shibell, the sheriff, hired Wyatt as deputy sheriff, which meant Wyatt had to quit riding shotgun on the stage and look around for a replacement.

He told Virge: "I wrote to Morg. Hell, he's just coolin' his heels in California, takin' a vacation. It's time he got back to work, and, besides, we can use him."

I was looking forward to seeing Lou again, but got a disappointment when Morg came in alone. Me, Bessie, and Mattie jumped on him like ducks on a June bug. "Where's Lou? Why didn't she come along?"

"Hold it! Hold it!" He held out his hands and shooed us off. "She's comin' as soon as she's on her feet. She's still not over the fever she caught up in Montana. We figured the climate and Ma's cooking would do her good a while longer."

I got the terrible notion that maybe she was dying and he didn't want to say. I remember dancing around coming right out with what I was thinking and can still hear myself saying: "It ain't . . . she ain't . . . ?" It was all I could get out.

He patted the top of my head like I was a school kid, and smiled. "She's not dyin', Allie. No more than the rest of us. And she sends her love. It's her legs mostly . . . sometimes her hands. She has days when it hurts to walk, but she's gettin' better. She'll probably come when the weather cools off." He wiped his face on his arm. "Is it always this damned hot here?"

Virge slapped him on the back. "The worst is over. June's the bad month. But it sure as hell beats freezin' in Deadwood by a jug full. The rainy season starts pretty soon and it cools off right smart, especially at night. Come on inside and tell us what Ma and Pa's been up to."

We had supper at our house that night, all of us crowded around the table, and me hoping the boys wouldn't take it in their heads to start a brawl for old times' sake and play rough house. I was relieved when they went off to show Morg the town and to do some gambling, and sat down with a thump. Morg had been right. It was damned hot.

"Must be a storm brewin'," Bessie said, fanning herself with her hand.

Mattie got up and opened the door, and we saw lightning far off over the Dragoons. "If it rains, I'll go stand in it," she said. "I'll go stomp barefoot in the puddles and sing. This damn' sun all the time gets to me."

There was another flash of lightning. I said: "You think Lou's all right? You think she'll ever get here?"

Bessie said: "Oh, she'll come. She's not goin' to leave a looker like Morg on his own for too long."

At that, Mattie let out a wail and put her face in her hands. Bessie got up and went to her. "What on earth is ailin' you?"

It took a while before Mattie could answer, and what she said was near as hurtful to us as to her. "It's Wyatt. He won't touch me. Hasn't for months. He's out all night, then comes home and goes to sleep. It's like I'm not even there." She took her hands away from her face and gave us a look like we was the ones doing wrong. "You wouldn't notice, of course. You got yours. I see how Jim looks at Bessie. How Virge is always touchin' you. How do you think I feel? Like a piece of damned furniture is how!"

I damned near said: *You brought it on yourself.*

Bessie was a lot kinder. "Honey . . . ," she started, using the motherly tone that she'd probably used on a lot of miserable girls in her time.

"Don't! I can't stand it!" There was an edge to Mattie's voice that said she was getting mad. "I might as well go back to work. At least I'd get paid for that."

159

"You can't," I said, and waited for the storm. It came all right.

"Don't you can't me, Allie Earp. That's all I hear from everybody. Can't, can't. Well, one of these days I'll do what I ~~god~~ damn' well please, and you won't stop me."

She went out, banging the door so hard I thought it'd come off its hinges. I looked at Bessie. "What'll we do with her?"

She sat with her chin in her hands, a frown on her face. "Nothin'. She made her bed and is lyin' in it. I had plenty of girls like her . . . stubborn and not too smart. Some of 'em died or killed themselves because they wouldn't listen to me or anybody else. She won't, either, and tryin' to talk sense or to help will just make her madder. We'll just have to let her run. Besides, it's not our problem. It's Wyatt's."

She was right about that. And a few months later, when a girl named Josephine Sarah Marcus blew into town, it was the beginning of the end for Mattie and for the rest of us. Of course, Josephine was our Sadie when she first came on the scene.

It wasn't too long after that when a Lieutenant Hurst from Fort Rucker came in looking for Virge. He had mounted infantry out there, and somebody had stolen a bunch of mules from the fort. He wanted Virge to find the rustlers and get the mules back. Stealing government property wasn't a joke, not then and not now.

Virge told Hurst to hang around a day or two while he tried to find out where the mules might have got to. That sort of news was apt to get out in a place like Tombstone. Everybody gossiped, and it was almost impossible to keep a secret, particularly with liquor loosening up mouths. Thank God none of the Earp boys ever drank much. Virge liked his beer, but Wyatt hardly ever drank, and Morg was like Virge.

Doc was the drinker in our crowd, and, when he finally blew in, his drinkin' was part of what led to our biggest trouble.

I told you Wyatt was working undercover for Wells Fargo, but I don't think I knew that then. Anyhow, one of the reasons Virge thought he could get a quick line on those mules was that he knew Wyatt already had a bunch of spies reporting to him on what was going on. Sure enough, that's how come Virge found out they was at the McLowery ranch over on the Babocamari, and he didn't waste time getting a posse together.

"You go stay with Jim and Bessie till I get back," he said to me. He was stuffing his pockets with extra rifle shells.

"Stayin' alone don't worry me. What does is what's in your pocket."

He put his hands on my shoulders. "It'll make my job easier if you just do what I tell you."

"And me sittin' here, worryin'."

He bent down and kissed me. "There's nothin' to worry over. Hell, I've got Wyatt, Morg, and Hurst along, though I wouldn't count on Hurst."

I sat around all day twiddling my thumbs, feeling real bad for the first time, and, by the time the door banged shut late that afternoon, I was ready to tell whoever it was to get some manners. But it was Virge, standing there, hot, tired, dust-covered, and mad.

"I need a bath," he said.

I went out back to get the tub where we kept it hanging beside the door. I'd just had the barrel filled, thank goodness. Real baths was a treat. Mostly we just washed off as best we could.

"What happened?" I asked him, ladling hot water out of the reservoir on the stove and dumping it in the tub, then adding a couple of pails from outside. "You find the mules?"

He was splashing water on his face—and every place else, too. "Hell, no, we didn't. Oh, they were there, all right. But Hurst's a damn' fool, and McLowery's a pretty smooth one. Said he'd make a deal with Hurst and give him back his mules if me or Wyatt didn't bring him in and jug him. Said they were on the place, but he'd have to send somebody to round 'em up. Wyatt said that was bullshit. Said he'd round up every critter on the place, but Hurst talked him out of it. If he didn't want me to do anything, he shouldn't have come to me in the first place. He doesn't have the smarts to deal with somebody like Frank McLowery. Talk won't get it. All Frank's kind understands comes out of a Forty-Five."

"Well, it ain't your fault." I handed him a towel. "Besides, it seems like a lot of fuss over a couple of old mules."

He tossed the towel down on the table. "This town, this whole part of the country's turnin' into a sewer. There's no telling what'll happen when men like McLowery get to thinkin' they're bigger than the law. What've we got to eat?"

"Bread and beans."

"Lay 'em on. I'm so hungry I could eat the ass end of a skunk. Then I got to go to the office and write out a report. And try not to make Hurst look dumber than he is. Can't figure how he ever got in the Army in the first place."

I watched him eat, watched him go off down the street, those long legs hitting the ground and stirring up dust.

A few days went by and Hurst got off what they called a "card" in the newspapers, cussing out Frank McLowery for double-crossing him by not giving back the mules, and calling him a crook. Frank McLowery shot back his own "card", calling Hurst a few names. They was both pretty safe doing that, with Hurst back at the fort and McLowery down on his ranch, about a hundred miles apart. But that wasn't the end of it.

A couple of days later Virge came in, slamming the door like he did when he was mad.

"Now what?" I said.

"That brassy bastard Frank McLowery had the nerve to come to my office and tell me I'd better not follow him again."

"He threatened you?" I could hardly believe what I was hearing. I mean, the law's the law, at least I'd always thought so. Tombstone sure was changing my mind on that subject, though.

"You could say that."

The idea of some rustler threatening Virge got my dander up. "I hope you tossed him out."

"Naw. He didn't really do anything, just mouthed off. I asked him if he was looking for a fuss."

And I knew just how Virge looked when he asked that. His eyes said it all. If that McLowery fella was smart, he'd have beat it out of there. "What'd he say?"

"Just said it all over, blustered around. So I told him to leave while the leavin' was good. He did. But he'll be back. He's a trouble-maker like that Clanton fella. Like I said, this place is fillin' up with scum. They're runnin' from the law and figure they're safe here."

"You think he'll make trouble?"

"You never know. He strikes me as a lot of wind."

Right there was where I started to worry every day, couldn't get to sleep at night sometimes. I had a bad feeling and it wasn't just the heebie-jeebies. My hunches about trouble had mostly turned out all my life. This wasn't going to be an exception, and this time it was in spades. Like I said, we should have left about then and hunted greener pastures. Either that or the boys should have stuck to gambling and business and forgot about the law. But it wasn't their way. So one of 'em would end up dead, and Virge crippled for life.

Chapter Twenty-Five

I've been reading that dude's fairy tale about how us women was cooped up in our houses and not allowed out, even in the daytime, and I have to laugh. The men, especially Virge and Morg, was crazy over the shows that came to town, and we'd have poisoned them if they'd left us home and went to one alone. They took us out to eat, too. Not to breakfast, like people do today, but noon and night. And there was an ice cream parlor where we could go, but always with the men, since it was over on Allen Street where the saloons was.

Of course, being married to gamblers and saloon men we was never invited out in what they call polite society today, but we didn't care. My idea of polite society in those days wasn't exactly printable—still isn't, come to think of it. Those women couldn't have harnessed a horse or shot a gun, if they had to, much less made a campfire, or cooked over one. Their men folks didn't stick up their noses at us, though. John Clum, after he got to be mayor and head of the Citizen's Safety Committee, used to come over to our house pretty often after supper, and ate with us more than once, and always complimented my cooking. And he stayed friends with the Earps long after the trouble in Tombstone was over.

I've got to explain that the Citizen's Safety Committee was really vigilantes, and the main reason Clum got acquainted with us Earps was that the Earp boys was the ones who did the vigilantes' dirty work. As vigilantes that committee was a joke. If they'd done their job, we wouldn't have had all the trouble we did.

Anyhow, Clum never put on the dog, and he talked to us polite as pie. Naturally he never brought his wife, and neither did Mr. Gage, or E.B. as everyone called him, but he came every once in a while to talk business with Virge. I don't wonder he went by his initials, since his front handle was Eliphalet. Usually Wyatt was at such confabs, too, when he was in town. He spent a lot of time out in the country after he got to be deputy sheriff.

I can still see us going out to a play at Ritchie's Hall in the evening, or maybe Schieffelin Hall after it got built, and even the Bird Cage, but it wasn't too polite a place to be seen. It was only open a few months before we left town. I don't remember the names of the plays we saw, but it didn't take much to entertain us in those days.

Folks would turn to watch us when we got to the theater, and I thought it was because we made such a handsome picture—the Earp boys wearing their city clothes and good shirts, Bessie in a ruffled dress and fancy hat, Mattie in blue that made her red hair even redder, and me in high-heeled, lace-up boots that always killed my feet!

Those traveling shows always drew a good crowd. Life was hard, and anything that promised fun, music, a break from work was welcome. So we rubbed elbows with miners, ranchers, storekeepers, gamblers and their flashy girl friends. Maybe that's why we got looked over. We was gamblers' ladies, too, come to think of it, and our men dressed us better than a lot of the other women.

If all we had to put up with in Tombstone was living like small town wives, it would've been a picnic. But I've already mentioned the gathering clouds—the likes of the Clantons and McLowerys, and Curly Bill on the way. Another low life that would join that crowd was John Ringo. Most came by way of Texas, whether they was Texans or not. Maybe the biggest cause of trouble was a bunch of crooks in what was called the Townlot Company. They got their fingers in the pot when the first mayor, Alder Randall, illegally turned over some of the best lots in town to them. I can't remember the details, but they tried to make people already living on those lots pay a fancy price. That was why John Clum started the vigilantes even before he was elected mayor. Hell, the Townlot Company even tried to make him pay for the lot his newspaper was on!

John had come to town after we did and started a paper called *The Epitaph*, saying every Tombstone needed an *Epitaph*. His paper started to take pot shots at the Townlot Company and soon enough at what he started calling the Cowboy Gang, a bunch of hardcases like the Clantons, Curly Bill, and the McLowerys and their followers.

It was after the Townlot Company got in business that I noticed the boys was going out at night and riding some of Wyatt's horses. I knew they wasn't going to gamble that way.

One night when I was sound asleep Virge woke me up, lighting a lamp in the bedroom.

I said: "What time is it?"

"Late."

"You been out late a lot. I know you been up to somethin'. What is it, if you don't mind tellin' me?"

At first he didn't want to tell me, but I kept staring at him until finally he opened up. "I guess it won't hurt so long as you don't let out a peep even to the other women."

"Shoot," I said.

He chuckled. "We been sorta movin' the Townlot Company's lot jumpers off their brand new lots."

"How?"

"We been lassoin' their tents and ridin' off with them."

"It sounds to me like a good way to get shot."

"Maybe. It's hard to shoot when your tent is draped around your neck, draggin' you around in horse turds and maybe a little cactus on the lots that're empty." He laughed again.

I thought that over while he took off his pants and shirt and tossed them on a chair, ready to get into bed. Naturally I asked what occurred to me. "You ain't doin' this free, I hope?"

"Not by a jug full."

That's when I first got an inkling that the town had an unofficial police force, and the boys was in on it. We had a marshal, Fred White, and he did all right and stuck up for the legal owners of the lots, but he was just one man, and he needed help. The respectable and prosperous businessmen who owned lots that they sure didn't want to pay for twice put up a kitty to hire some help for him, and that's where Virge and his brothers came in. Warren was in town by then, too. He'd been home helping out Ma and Pa Earp, but the letters from his brothers were too much for him, and he came to get in on the fun.

Somewhere along in there Doc Holliday and Kate came to town. We'd left them in Prescott, but he'd been roaming around, including a stop in Las Vegas where he shot somebody and had to pull his freight. I wasn't sure what had happened to her or even if they was still together.

I was cutting up a chicken and wondering if I could get

some buttermilk from Chandler's milk ranch just outside of town, when somebody knocked at the door, and there Kate was, pretty as a picture and holding out her arms.

"Where'd you come from? Just like a bad penny, turnin' up out of nowhere!" I hugged her close.

"I've been everywhere." She took off her hat, a fancy little thing trimmed with white feathers, and laid it on the table. "Colorado with my brothers, Iowa with my sisters, and back to Prescott. It's like I said before. I don't belong anywhere except with Doc."

"Is that so bad?"

"I think so. He'd rather be with the Earps, with Wyatt, than with me."

"Don't he love you?" I had to ask, although I reckoned I knew the answer.

She gave a shrug. "Who knows? I don't. We suit very well in bed and even sometimes out of it. Except . . . he can't forget what I was and doesn't want to. He doesn't realize I couldn't help what I did. He's only a man, after all. It's women who know how hard it is."

"You ain't gonna change him."

"I know." Her eyes, blue with lavender around the edges, was sad. "And I wouldn't want him different. Maybe just healthy. But I want a home. A family. He doesn't, or doesn't want it with me. I came down here with him, mostly to see you, but I'm not staying. At least not for long."

"Does he know?"

"Not yet. I'll tell him when the time is right."

"Where you goin'? Wherever it is, don't lose touch. We all missed you."

"Did you?" Her face crumpled. "I didn't think anyone ever missed me. Even my sisters seemed . . ."—she searched for the word—"like strangers. And I found I didn't belong back in their world any more. Maybe I never did. I want to be with Doc, but I won't live in Wyatt's pocket. And Mattie won't ever be able to forget what was between me and Wyatt."

Well, she was right on that count, but I wanted a happy reunion even if Mattie's nose did get out of joint. "I saw Doc's face when you lost the baby, and he thought you was dyin'. He looked like he'd lost his only friend."

She smiled, kind of amused. "Friend? Of course, I'm his friend. And his mother. His sister. His lover. All of those, but it's not enough. Do you know what it's like to be not enough? To know you can't replace what's been taken away or lost?"

I swear, she set me back on my heels. When she said that, I saw us all, each and every one of us—Virge and me close as two vines growing together, and the same with Bessie and Jim, and Morg and Lou. We, none of us, had lost nothing that kilt off our spirits, and we'd found out how to keep on growing. It was Kate's pain that Doc couldn't forget she'd been a whore. It was damned hard, and a damned shame.

"Let's forget it for now," I said. "How about coffee? And I'll call Bessie and Mattie over for a get-together."

Her eyes was wise-looking, wiser than her years. "I'd like that, Allie. Very much."

She didn't hang around long. A couple weeks later she was gone on the stage to Globe and left Doc on his own. To tell the truth, he wasn't happy about it, started drinking more than was good for him. He cared more than he let on to her or to anybody else, and I kind of wished he'd grow up and settle down. In his case, that was asking too much. Pride's what it was, and, the way I saw it, pride always led to a fall.

Chapter Twenty-Six

Early in August I went to Temecula where Virge's ma and pa were running a hotel at the Hot Springs. Lou had been missing Morg as bad as he missed her, but she didn't want to make the trip to Tombstone by herself. I got a shock when I laid eyes on her. Whatever fever she'd caught up there in Montana had changed her forever. Her eyes was sunk, and her face seemed like it was just skin over bone. But for all that, she was more beautiful than before, as if she'd cheated death and was lit up from inside on account of it.

When I asked Ma Earp what was the matter, she just shook her head. "If I knew, I'd fix it. She's got good days and bad ones, and there's no tellin' when the bad ones come on. Soakin' in the springs does her a little good, but she's pinin' after Morg. Maybe bein' with him'll help, though I doubt it."

Like Ma said, Lou had her good days, when she walked me around and showed me the flowers and the trees, and named 'em all, and filled the air with that silvery laugh of hers. But there was other times when she was hurting and stayed close to home, wrapped in a shawl, and nothing any of us did seemed to help.

Toward the end of the month, Virge came over. "I been

missin' my bride," was how he put it. "And my ma's cookin'!"

I believed him on both counts, for his ma was the best cook I ever run across. I spent a lot of time just following her around, watching what she cooked, and how she babied her bread dough, sometimes talking to it like it could hear, and giving it an extra pat before putting it in the oven. She had herbs growing everywhere, too, things I never heard of, and she used them in the kitchen and for healing, too. I wish I'd known half of what that old woman knew. She could cure most anything, and till the end of her days she fussed about not being able to help Lou.

Virge hadn't been there long when he said: "Tomorrow I'm takin' you girls on an excursion." And when we wanted to know where, he just grinned and looked sly. "It's a surprise."

We left early in the morning, Lou and me all excited. It was one of her good days, and we gabbled and chattered like a pair of magpies, not noticing where we was going, although it was a long way across the hills.

Virge finally pulled up and looked back at us, his eyes twinkling with that light I always loved. "Here you are," he said. "What you wished for back in Council Bluffs. What d'you think?"

To tell the truth, I couldn't think at all, just sat there staring like a ninny. Some things are so big, so grand, that just seeing 'em is like getting punched in the stomach, and that's how I felt at my first sight of the ocean. All that water that went clear to the other side of the world, and all the colors in it from blue and gray to green when the waves spilled over, and the wind blowing in our faces, sharp and salty.

"Well, what've you got to say?"

I shook my head, not taking my eyes off the water.

"Nothin'. Nothin' at all." I could've sat there for a week, but Lou grabbed my hand.

"Come on. Let's hunt for shells." She was funny that way, always collecting stuff—leaves, flowers, grasses—and pressing 'em in books or sending 'em home to her sisters. And when we got back to Tombstone, she like to wore us all out hunting for cactus and desert plants.

What I did first was plunk down in the sand and take off my boots and stockings. Then I hitched up my skirt and stuck my bare feet in the water. Lord, it was cold! But I loved doing it, loved running along the edge, Virge chasing after me, barefooted, too, both of us yelling and splashing like we was five years old. Oh, we had our fun, but it was too soon over. All of it.

Tombstone was pretty quiet when we got back, although the Cowboy Gang, as now everybody had started calling 'em, was coming into town regular. For a while, though, the town was fairly peaceful. Wyatt was doing a good job as deputy sheriff—a better job than Fred White was doing as marshal. Fred didn't have the experience, and I never did figure why Tombstone picked him for the job. He was popular, though, and brave enough, and that's what got him killed the night of October 27, 1880.

We didn't know it at the time, but learned soon enough, that the shooting had been a set-up. Fred White had sided with the people against the Townlot Company, which included Mike Gray, and Mike had a ranch over in the Animas Valley right next to Curly Bill and Old Man Clanton. It makes sense that Mike hired himself a killer to get rid of Fred who stood in his way. Mike was a hardcase, had been a Texas Ranger, and had probably killed plenty himself. Don't get me wrong. The Texas Rangers did a hell of a good job, bringing law and order, but when one of 'em went bad, he did it up brown. His part in the Townlot thing shows Mike Gray up as no damned good. But I'm getting ahead of myself again. Like I keep saying, the whole Tombstone trouble was a tangle, and unraveling it's not easy, especially after sixty years.

But on the night of the killing, a bunch of cowboys was up around Sixth and Frémont shooting the moon and making a ruckus. Wyatt and Morg was down at Vogan's where Jim was tending bar, and went out to see what was happening, but Fred White had got there first. He was facing Curly Bill, telling him to hand over his pistol, when Wyatt grabbed Curly from behind. White was cussing Curly and grabbed the pistol which went off and nailed him. Now I know enough about six-shooters to know the damned thing was cocked if it went off that way. Why did Curly have a cocked pistol in his hand in the first place? Shooting the moon like he said? That's bullshit. Anyhow, Wyatt knocked Curly cold, laying his pistol barrel alongside his head, and, when he woke up, Wyatt dragged him down to the J.P.'s. The funny thing about that is that Mike Gray was the J.P., and we always wondered how he felt having to bind over his own gunman.

Later I heard Virge ask Wyatt: "What in hell was Curly doin' right out in front of White's cabin?"

Wyatt gave him a look. "Seems like you should already know the answer."

"Yeah, but I can't prove it."

"Neither can I, but it stands to reason. And while we're talking about it, we'd better watch our own backs."

Virge pulled on his mustache. "Hell, we been doing that since we were kids."

Watching the two of 'em, I reckoned Virge spoke the truth.

There was another tangle in the story that only us Earps knew about, us and a few others who weren't about to spill the beans. Wells Fargo was behind the Earps all the way. They planned to put their men in law jobs all over southeast Arizona and just about that time had backed Bob Paul for sheriff of Pima County. He lost the election to Charlie Shibell, but Wyatt thought the election had been rigged. Seems like somebody over in the Cowboy country near San Simon had stuffed the ballot box. Not too hard to figure with over 100 votes where only a dozen or so people really lived.

Wyatt figured Curly Bill could give him the testimony to prove all this, and he made a deal with him. He promised to get him off on Fred White's killing, if Curly got his friends to testify when Paul sued Shibell over a crooked election. Mind, I heard all this around the house then, and around lots of other houses and even campfires over the years when the boys lived it all over. Let's face it. Wyatt was a hard man, and so was Virge, and there's nothing wrong with that. As lawmen, they was honest as the day is long. But I can still hear Wyatt saying: "Fred was a damn' greenhorn, and shouldn't have tried to ramrod a town like Tombstone in the first place. I'm surprised he lasted as long as he did. But we wanted Bob Paul in as sheriff, and to do that I had to prove the election was illegal. I did it my way."

Doing it his way meant that he took Curly to Tucson and testified to the judge that Curly's pistol was defective and would go off on half cock, proving the shooting was an accident. But as Virge said later: "The hammer might drop on half cock, but a Colt doesn't have enough steam in the hammer spring to make it shoot when it only drops less'n halfway. Besides that, what the hell was Curly doing with six rounds in the chamber if he wasn't loaded for bear? We all carried those old Colts on an empty round. The son-of-a-bitch shoved in an extra going into a fight."

Wyatt nodded. "Sure. But the judge didn't know that. He was a city guy. Probably never shot a gun in his life."

"Some judge," was all that Virgil said.

After White was killed, Virge was marshal for a few days, but then they had a special election, and another damned city guy, Ben Sippy, got the job. Tombstone had a hell of a time learning its lesson about lawmen. Virge ran again in January, 1881 and lost again to Sippy, who was a damned fool and didn't have what it took to handle a town like that one.

That was the year that Johnny Behan and Sadie got there, too, although then she was Josephine Marcus and engaged to Johnny. He came sometime in the summer and worked as a bartender, then opened a livery stable with John Dunbar, another loose one. Sadie came later, and told me she got there the night Fred White was shot, and heard the shooting, which gave her a bad first impression of the place. It was the right impression, though, come to think of it.

She'd met Johnny the year before when the theater troupe she'd run away with was playing in Prescott. Now, she never did say why a girl from a well-off Jewish family in San Francisco decided to leave home and be an actress. She had a lot of secrets and kept 'em, but I always figured she'd been soft on some actor and went after him. Then she met Johnny, and his Irish blarney sweet-talked her into hitching up with him. He convinced her to come to Tombstone to get married, and even got around her family, which must have taken some doing.

But Johnny wasn't about to marry anybody. He was just interested in taking what he could get from her and everybody else. He'd always been a two-bit politician and knew the Democratic sharks up in Prescott were angling to make a new county with Tombstone as the county seat. Tombstone was all for it, too. So, although he tended bar and opened a livery stable, he was already planning to make a killing in another office where he could fleece the taxpayers, and that's exactly what he did.

Chapter Twenty-Seven

It was a while after Fred was killed that I first saw Sadie. She was walking down the street, holding a little boy by the hand.

"Who's that?" I asked Virge. We was coming back from the ice cream parlor.

He told me, then said as how she was engaged to Behan and was taking care of his kid.

"He's got a kid?" I was surprised, not that I knew much about Behan then.

"Yeah. He's divorced. Heard he beat up his first wife pretty bad, and was foolin' around on her, too. That's just gossip, but she did divorce him up in Prescott."

"Does this Miss Marcus know she's engaged to a wife beater?" I felt like crossing the street and whispering the truth in her ear. She seemed so happy with the kid, and he with her, it was a shame.

"It's not my business or yours," he said.

Well, it wasn't, but it didn't seem right to let that gal walk into trouble with no warning. Still, she found out about Johnny on her own, then walked into trouble with Wyatt, her eyes wide open. And I have to say they was beautiful eyes, dark brown with thick black lashes. I always envied her those eyelashes, seeing as mine was hardly noticeable. I never envied her life with Wyatt, though. Not with Mattie's ghost always hanging there.

In those days, Mattie was always fussing. It was Wyatt this, and Wyatt that, till I could hardly stand being around her. "He takes care of you, don't he?" I asked her one day.

"I've got a roof over my head," she snapped out. "But there's nobody under it with me. Wyatt's hardly ever around, and, when he is, he don't say two words."

Well, Wyatt wasn't the jolliest fella I ever met, and I never heard him guffaw like Virge was always doing, but he had a soft heart for those that needed help, and I know he felt Mattie needed him. But there was always that other side of him—cold as ice—and that's what got us in trouble. He and his brothers shouldered the law even when it wasn't their job. They just saw what needed doing and did it. Like the time Johnny-Behind-the-Deuce, a two-bit gambler whose real name I can't recall, shot a man down in Charleston. They said he had good reason, but he wasn't popular there, and the dead man had a lot of friends who decided on a hanging. The constable got Johnny in a buggy and headed for Tombstone, but somebody spotted 'em slipping out, and a bunch took after 'em. Virge was out on the Charleston road that afternoon, moving one of Wyatt's racehorses and spotted the buggy coming hell for leather. He rode up alongside, found out the trouble, and got close enough for Johnny to jump on the horse behind him.

Even carrying double, that big thoroughbred could run, and Virge came into Tombstone a half mile ahead of the mob. He went straight to Vogan's, figuring he'd find Wyatt there. The boys hung out at Vogan's, since Jimmy was tending bar. He was in luck, 'cause Morg and Warren was there, too.

They got organized real quick, stuck Johnny inside, and

hustled the customers out so they wouldn't get plugged if lead started flying. By the time the mob got there, Wyatt and Virge was outside with scatter-guns, and Jimmy and Warren Earp was inside with rifles. Like always, the regular law, Marshal Sippy and Deputy Sheriff Behan, wasn't nowhere to be found. By the time they showed up, the Earp boys had convinced the mob somebody'd get killed trying to take Johnny away.

Behan and Sippy got a wagon to take the prisoner to Tucson, and the boys escorted them out of town. I remember Warren coming on the run to get his horse and finding me out front, wondering what all the shouting was about. I never gave a thought to the fact I could get picked off by accident if shooting started. I was just being nosey.

Warren yelled at me: "For God's sake, get in the house and keep away from the windows!"

I just stood there with my mouth open, and he finally came up and shoved me through the door. "Just do what I told you. That crowd could flare up again, and you standin' here waitin' to get shot or run over."

Well, when he was gone, I peeked out anyhow, saw the wagon leaving and the boys riding alongside, looking like grim death. That mob didn't cause any more trouble, and they got Johnny in the jug in Tucson. The funny thing about that was that he escaped, and nobody ever saw him again. I reckon he was smarter than most.

But after that, it seemed, everything speeded up. Seeing it again in my mind, it's like standing and watching a train go past—fast, and not caring a hoot for what's in its way.

Early in 1881, the new county was finally split off from Pima County. They named it Cochise after the Apache Injun chief. I've always felt that dead Injun put a curse on the place and everybody in it for stealing his home and kicking his people out, and nothing ever happened to change my mind. Wyatt was Wells Fargo's pick to be the first sheriff of the new county, but that little bastard, Behan, was in tight with Governor Frémont and wanted the job himself. He was always looking for ways to stick his fingers in the pot. But just to make sure, he rigged a deal with Wyatt, promising him the job as under-sheriff. Wyatt worked it out with Wells Fargo, and then Johnny double-crossed him and gave the job to Harry Woods. Why? We all knew why, 'cause by that time Sadie had figured Johnny out and set her cap for Wyatt.

A long time later she told me the whole story—about why she kicked Johnny out of the house they was living in—the house she'd damned well bought and paid for. Little Albert, Johnny's kid, was hard of hearing, and she'd taken him to a doctor in San Francisco to see if anything could be done to help. I'll give her this. She was a good mother to the kid, and he loved her. They stayed friends always, visiting each other and keeping in touch, and, if Albert turned out fine, it was 'cause of Sadie.

Anyhow, she came back early, figuring on surprising Johnny and maybe having a little romantic reunion. Telling about it, she was still mad as all get out, her dark eyes flashing.

"I surprised him, all right. With Kitty Jones. My best friend! In my bed! My house! I'm surprised you didn't hear me. I chased them out, still pulling on their clothes. Oh"—she gave a snort—"he came back and tried to make it right. Had all kinds of sweet talk and reasons, but I'd had my eyes opened. All the way. I was through with him. If I'd thought, I'd have shot him and saved us all a lot of trouble. But I was worried about Albert. He was such a dear boy."

Not long after Sadie broke up with Johnny, Mattie came

over one morning, her eyes all red from crying, her hair
sticking out every which way. She banged the door and
started pacing around the room. "Wyatt hasn't been comin'
home at night at all," she said, and I swear I heard her teeth
grinding. "Not for weeks, and I know what the son-of-a-
bitch is doin'."

"Best sit and tell me." Her switching around was enough
to make me start grinding my own teeth.

"He's with that bitch of Behan's."

Why wasn't I surprised? Wyatt always had an eye for a
good-looking woman, and half the men in town, including
Doc, was sniffing around the girl now that she was through
with Johnny. She wasn't any better than she should be, but
she was beautiful, and she didn't charge for it.

"I got an anonymous letter sayin' so. I think Behan
wrote it."

I thought about that, putting two and two together.
Behan had backed out of giving Wyatt the job as under-
sheriff right after he and Sadie split. He was surely damned
mad and jealous, to boot, and, besides, every man in town
was laughing at him for losing his woman. Hell, there's
nothing worse than a man who's been dumped by a woman,
and Johnny was always a damned vicious little hater.

"It figures," I said. "The double-crossing little bastard."

"They're both bastards. All men are bastards." She put
her head on her arms on the table and bawled.

I felt terribly sorry for her, but there wasn't a damned
thing I could do except let her cry it out and be there when
she was done. What goes on between men and women in
bed oughtn't to have a place in what happens in the world
or in politics, but it does, and it ruined our chances in
Tombstone and changed our lives forever. Proving my
point, I remember Jimmy saying once: "Hell, we'd all have

got on well there if Wyatt had kept his pecker in his pants."

Not a one of us laughed.

Mattie and I was still sitting there, me trying to think how to cheer her, when Lou came in, all bright-eyed. She was having one of her good days, and I sure welcomed the sight of her.

"Morg's takin' me out to look for cactuses," she said, not noticing Mattie's swollen face. "Come with us, and let's have a picnic."

"I'm stayin' here." Mattie's head was so full of tears she sounded like she was underwater.

Lou shot me a look of understanding. "No, you aren't," she said. "It won't be any fun without you."

At that, I rolled my eyes, and got a good frown from Lou.

"Please," Lou said. "Let's just all be together. I feel good, the sun's out, and . . . oh, please, let's go."

Well, it'd take a stone to resist Lou when she was like that. I jigged Mattie's arm. "Come on. Wash your face, grab your bonnet, and we'll get the hell out of here for a while. I'll get the lunch."

Outnumbered, she got up. "I might as well. For sure he won't be home any time soon."

"What's the matter now?" Lou asked when she'd gone.

I told her, and she sat down in the empty chair. "Poor thing. She's hung on this long, but I guess I knew it'd happen someday. Look at her. Then look at the Marcus girl. She's different. Sophisticated. Beautiful."

"Not as beautiful as you."

That laugh floated out, but I heard sadness in it. "I was. Once. Not any more. But thanks. And thanks for sayin' you'd come. Maybe we can make her forget, at least for today."

We didn't have no luck with Mattie, or with finding Lou's cactuses, either, but it was good getting out, and Lou found something she called verbena, and got Morg to dig it up and put it in a little box to send to her sister.

Mattie watched them, then said: "What's the point? It'll just die."

"Agnes will take care of it and make it bloom." Lou was positive.

"Fussin' over a damn' plant. All for nothing." Her voice was as bitter as quinine.

Lou started to say something, then bit her lip and turned away, but I wondered if she wasn't thinking the same thing I was. That without caring, there's no way in the world anything can grow or bloom, and that included Mattie.

Both Kate and Bat Masterson was in town the night the Kinnear stage was held up. Kate was there because Doc had written, saying he missed her, and nothing would do but she had to leave Globe and come running. For once, though, they seemed to be getting along, and I hadn't seen too much of her. But that night Doc was gambling, and Kate and Bessie was at my place. We was sitting around the stove after supper, me with my mending and Bessie knitting on a sweater—seems she was always knitting—and then Virge ran in.

"Bob Paul just called from Benson. The Kinnear stage was held up, and Bud Philpot's dead. We're goin' out there." He pulled on his heavy coat. "Don't wait up." Then he was gone.

Kate lifted an eyebrow. "Does he really think you'll go to sleep?"

"He don't think. He just does his job," I said, knowing

I'd not shut my eyes till he got home.

"Poor Allie."

I was already riding with 'em in the dark, the cold March wind blowing in my face, the mountains darker than the sky, and trouble waiting. "We been lucky so far."

Kate clicked her tongue. "Never trust to luck. It's the big betrayer."

The hold-up had happened at a place called Drew's Station down beyond Contention. Bob Paul was supposed to be riding shotgun, but had taken the reins 'cause the regular driver, Bud Philpot, was under the weather. Without any warning, a bunch of outlaws jumped the stage and shot Philpot, then took off without taking the money box. It doesn't take a fortune-teller to figure out what they was up to. It wasn't a hold-up at all, but a put-up job to get rid of Paul. In the dark they'd shot the wrong man. Remember, Paul was suing Charlie Shibell over that rigged election, and it looked like he was gonna win his case, and by that time the outlaws was organized enough they didn't want to see someone like Paul as sheriff. Hell, they was running wild all over that part of the country, stealing and killing, and everybody knew it.

The boys formed a posse next morning and took off after the outlaws. They brought back one of 'em, a fella named Luther King. He wasn't in Behan's jail long. The fact is, he had the run of the place while he was there, and one day, while he was with Harry Woods, he just walked out the back door, jumped on a horse that was waiting there for him, and rode off.

I'd cooked supper for the boys and their friend, Bat Masterson, that night. He'd been one of the posse, and I liked him. He was an interesting man, and I'd bet he never backed down from anything that was thrown at him. Although they ate like they was starving, I could feel the tension in each one of 'em, that and anger. They was mad clear through.

Without warning, Wyatt slammed down his fork. "It's plain that son-of-a-bitch Behan and Harry Woods let King go. Probably afraid he'd squeal on them."

"If it'd been up to Johnny, we'd never have caught him in the first place," Morg said.

"How come?" I couldn't resist asking but got a mind-your-own-business look from Virge.

Morg ignored him, and gave me a grin. "I'll tell you if I can have another piece of pie."

I cut a piece and set it in front of him, but he didn't touch it right away, just told the story for me and the other women who was all ears.

"In the first place, it wasn't a hold-up. They were after Bob Paul and made a mistake. It was dark, and Paul wasn't supposed to be drivin', so they got the wrong man. In the second place, by the time we got there, any trail they'd left had been messed up, and there was Behan sayin' it was no use chasin' after whoever it was. It seemed like him and his flunky Breckenridge both wanted whoever it was to get away."

"But you caught one," I said, not caring if I was interrupting.

"Yeah. We tracked him to Redfield's ranch down on the San Pedro. He came out and gave us some story about how he was workin' there, but he was carryin' two pistols and enough cartridges, so we doubted that. Then Wyatt and Bob Paul figured out a way to scare him into talkin'."

Wyatt gave one of his laughs that had no fun in it. "And I have to say it worked. We took King inside and told him Kate was in that stage and had got shot. Said Doc was comin' after whoever killed his woman, and King started singin' like a canary. Gave us three names. Billy Leonard, Harry Head, and Jim Crane."

I could believe that fella was scared. Doc's reputation—and his temper—was enough to scare hell out of the worst hardcase.

"But Paul said there were eight of 'em," Virge put in. "You have any idea who the others were?"

Wyatt put his hands on the table and studied 'em a minute. Then he said: "Yeah, I think I know, and sooner or later I'll prove it. If that skunk Woods hadn't let King walk, I'd have sweated the rest out of him. But at least now we know who we're lookin' for."

Bat had been part of the posse, but, listening to the boys, he shook his head. "I thought Dodge City was bad. I hate to stick my nose in, but after what I been seein', if I was you, I'd look for greener pastures."

The trouble with that was the Citizen's Safety Committee and Wells Fargo was paying the boys every month, and money was rolling in. They'd got a belly full of nice guys like Fred White, and weaklings like Sippy, not to mention crooks like Behan, and had hired the toughest men around to run the law end.

I agreed with Bat, though, and in bed that night I said to Virge: "We oughta get out of here. It ain't a good place. I feel like we're caught in a spider web with all the crooks and killers just waitin' their chance."

He laughed it off. "This is our chance to make our taw. We'll never have a better one, and I'm expectin' our mines to pay off, too."

Well, I was right, and he was wrong. In less than a year we'd hit the road a lot sadder and wiser.

Chapter Twenty-Eight

Virge was waving at me a copy of *The Nugget*, the other town paper, and cussing like I never heard come out of him. Harry Woods, who owned the paper and who was one of Behan's toadies as well as being under-sheriff, had printed a story accusing Doc Holliday of robbing the stage and killing Bud Philpot. The trouble was that folks got to believing what was in the paper, and other papers took it up, even though the whole thing was an out-and-out lie. The big problem was proving it, although a lot of folks knew Doc had been in town gambling that night and he had witnesses to say so.

"It's that bastard Behan again," Virge was saying. "He wants to keep Wyatt from running in the next election, and that chicken-shit Woods'll do anything to help him."

"Why Doc?" I asked, although I figured I knew the answer, which was that, if Wyatt couldn't clear his friend, he didn't stand a chance in an election.

"Hell fire, why not Doc? Behan wants to get rid of him and us, too."

Get rid of? To me that meant killing, and I shivered. "I don't like any of this."

He patted my shoulder, and I got the feeling he'd forgot I was there. "It'll be all right," he said. "Don't worry."

Of course, I worried. How could I help it, not knowing who to trust or when the next trouble would come? And then one morning Kate showed up, looking a fright. One of her eyes was black and swelled shut, and she had a bruise alongside her jaw that was turning purple.

"Lord save us! What happened?" She had blood on her clothes and dried on her face. I sat her down and started dipping some water into a basin.

"He beat hell out of me! That little. . . ." She said something in Hungarian that sounded bad.

"Doc?" I was astonished. No matter what, Doc was a gentleman, not the kind to beat up women.

"Behan. He got me drunk."

That figured. Hell, like Virge told me, he was a wife beater from away back, but why would he do such a thing to Kate? "Close your eyes," I said. "I'm gonna wash the blood off your face. Don't say nothin' till I'm done."

She cursed again, started crying, and then the whole rotten story came out. She and Doc had had a fight—nothing new there—and she was standing outside, trying to calm down, when Behan came along. He took her to supper, bought her drinks, and got her drunk, then took her to a hotel and beat her till she signed a paper, saying Doc had been in on the stage hold-up. Of course, he had his own rotten purpose, which was to get rid of all of us.

The problem was, Kate had been so drunk and in so much pain she didn't know what she was putting her name to and didn't care as long as he stopped using her for a punching bag. When Wyatt heard her story, he got a look on his face I'll never forget. He was fire and ice, full of an anger that went so deep I hoped I'd never see it again. I did, though, more times than I want to remember.

He dragged Kate down to testify that none of what was

on that paper was true, and in the end Doc got off, but it took till June. I was surprised Doc didn't go out and kill Behan, but he was so damned mad at Kate he wasn't thinking and went on a drunk instead. And when Doc went on a drunk, it was a good one.

"You tell Doc I said good bye." Kate was leaving for Globe. "I can't trust myself to see him. He makes me crazy. I make him crazy." She blew her nose. "We don't love. We hate."

"Maybe they're the same thing."

She squinted at me out of her good eye. "Then pity us all."

I was in bed but not sleeping when the boys came in, talking low so as not to wake me. To tell the truth, I was feeling lazy and didn't get up, just lay there, listening. And I got an earful!

Virge said: "You can't trust Ike Clanton. Sure he wants the reward for the hold-up, but how do you know he's not layin' for you?"

"I'll take the chance." Wyatt's voice was flat, and I knew just how he looked, sitting there at the table—like a wolf on the hunt. "Ike's welcome to the reward as long as I get to bring in Leonard, Head, and Crane. I'll get the truth out of 'em one way or another and clear Doc. Kate's gettin' in that mess with Behan didn't help much." The chair squeaked like he'd pushed himself back. "That woman makes trouble every time she gets anywhere near Doc."

"And trusting Ike might get you in trouble, Brother." Virge was worried. I could hear it.

"Like I said, I'll risk it. I've wasted enough time trailin' those three. Let's see if Ike can bring 'em in where I've got a chance at 'em."

Lying there, I put two and two together. Somehow Ike Clanton and Wyatt had made a deal where, in exchange for fingering the three men involved in the Kinnear stage hold-up, Ike would get the reward money Wells Fargo offered, and Wyatt would clear Doc's name and his own. It made sense except for one thing, and Virge'd put his finger on it. Nobody with any sense could take Ike's word for anything. He was running with the Cowboy Gang and up to his neck in every crooked affair in the county.

Next morning I said to Virge: "You goin' along with that scheme? I heard you talkin' last night."

"I might've guessed." He gave me a smile, but his eyes was serious. "I reckon I'll have to. It's Wyatt's call, and he's dead set on it."

"You don't trust Ike?"

"I'd sooner trust a rattlesnake. But you know Wyatt. He's got his mind made up and nobody's going to stop him. He's got to clear Doc and himself, or else."

Nobody did stop Wyatt, either. He'd gone out a couple times, trailing those three that King had named, and had come back empty-handed. And then came the news that Leonard and Head had got themselves killed over in Hachita. God knows what they was doing. I can't recall, but it wasn't anything good. That still left Jim Crane out there somewhere, though, and Wyatt dead set on finding him.

What I remember of that time is that it rained nearly every day, the roads was turned to mud, and my house stank like the underside of a mushroom. Just to complicate things, Geronimo had jumped the reservation, and the Apaches was raiding all over that part of the country. Even folks in town was afraid that maybe they'd come in on a raid. They never did, but we was all strung tight as a wire worrying.

And then Wyatt, Morg, Warren, Doc and some others left town and didn't come home. It wasn't unusual for Wyatt to be gone a couple days, but with the others gone, too, it only made the strain worse. It wasn't an easy time for us women. Lou popped in one afternoon all fussed. "Mattie's stealin' my pain medicine," she said after checking to see if I was alone.

"Figures."

"She must've come over to Bessie's a couple times when I wasn't there. I asked her about it, but she denied doin' anything."

"Why'd she have to steal from you? Hell, she could buy what she wants anywhere."

Lou looked at me, unhappy. "I'm not sure she isn't doing that, too, the way she's been actin'."

"You want me to talk to her?" I knew that was useless as soon as I said it, and shook my head. "That won't do no good. Let me talk to Virge."

Lou had on a bright-colored Mexican shawl, and she was fooling with the fringe, braiding and unbraiding it. "I'm scared. Everything's a mess. Morg and Wyatt gone all the time, never sayin' why or where they're going, and Mattie sittin' there starin' at the wall. I'm scared, and I don't know what to do."

"Nothin' we can do." I remembered Melissa's words from what seemed a hundred years before: *It's men who do the fighting. Women stay home and worry.*

Her eyes filled up with tears. "If anything happens to Morg. . . ."

"You got to believe it won't. Keep cheerful for him. Worryin' about us only makes it harder on them."

I sounded braver than I was, but she smiled through her tears. "You hold us all together, bless you."

"If I do, it ain't my fault!"

We both laughed and felt a mite better.

That night I got hold of Virge and told him about Mattie. For the first time ever, he damned near snapped my head off. "Don't bother me about her! She's Wyatt's damn' problem. I've got enough to worry about!"

"What?" I was bristling in spite of myself.

"Like where in hell my brothers are."

"You don't know?"

He never answered, just put on his hat and walked out the door. I always got mad as hell when he did that, for all the good it did me.

He didn't have to say. Word came in that Old Man Clanton had got killed by Mexicans in a place called Skeleton Cañon—the old man, Jim Crane, Dixie Gray, Mike's club-foot son, and some others. And about a week after that, Wyatt came in at night alone looking like he'd been dragged through hell.

Turned out he and his posse, looking for Jim Crane, had run across Old Man Clanton and some others, including Crane, driving a herd of stolen cattle. They laid for 'em, hoping to catch Crane, but the rustlers started shooting— and got killed for doing it.

Warren got shot in the shoulder, and Doc caught it in the leg, but somehow Wyatt and the posse had sneaked 'em both over to Deming and put Morg and Warren on a train for California. Doc went off somewhere to heal up his leg. I think he met his pa in New Orleans, but for damned sure neither he nor Warren was going to show themselves in town in the condition they was in with Old Man Clanton and his bunch dead.

Tombstone was buzzing with speculation and gossip. At first the word had been that Mexicans pulled off that shooting, and that was partly right. There was Mexican soldiers down there, aiming to put a stop to rustling across the line. Marshal Dake, who Virge worked for, had been dickering with the Mexicans and was behind sending in Wyatt's posse, and so was Wells Fargo. They was as anxious to get rid of the outlaws down in that country as anybody.

The trouble was that a lot of folks had noticed that the Earps and Doc and their crowd had been out of town at about that time. There was talk, and the Clanton boys got suspicious. I had a hunch we was in for it, and I wasn't wrong.

Chapter Twenty-Nine

Sometime that September the Bisbee stage was held up. The hold-up men got the strongbox and a bunch of loot off the passengers. It didn't take long for Wyatt to find out who did it. He and Morg, who'd got back from California, brought in Frank Stillwell and Pete Spence and booked 'em. Of course, they was out on bond quick, the reason being that Frank was one of Behan's deputies. It showed Behan up for just what kind of sheriff he was with friends and cops like Frank working for him. It's a wonder nobody high up ever caught on to what he was doing, but they never did, and it was left to the boys to do what they could.

After that the Cowboys got nervous. Frank McLowery even threatened Morg, saying he'd get him for arresting Stillwell, and Ike Clanton got to feeling guilty about his deal with Wyatt that fingered Leonard, Head, and Crane. He was worried his gang would find out what he'd done, and he'd be in real trouble. Ike's problem was, like with most of them, that he wasn't smart. Hell, I don't think any of the Cowboys had what you could call a brain. Probably Old Man Clanton was the smart one, but with him dead, there wasn't anybody telling Ike and his bunch what to do.

Doc had come back from wherever he went in October, and had somehow gone to Globe and made up with Kate. I tell you, those two couldn't ever make up their minds, couldn't live alone, couldn't live together, just like Kate said. There was times I sure felt sorry for both of 'em. About then, he took her to the *fiesta* in Tucson to do some gambling, and wired Wyatt where he was. Good thing, too. Somebody tipped Wyatt off that Ike and his whole crowd was coming in for a showdown.

"If there's going to be a fight, we want Doc here," Wyatt said, and sent Morg to Tucson to tell him what was going on and make sure he came back.

"What's goin' to happen?" I asked Virge, not happy with how things looked.

"Whatever happens, we'll take care of it. You just stick close to home."

Like I said, the boys was lawmen above all else. They was paid to keep the law, and to take care of those who didn't, and, no matter how black that writer tried to paint 'em, making 'em out to be stagecoach robbers and killers and all, there's no getting away from the fact that they did their duty.

It wasn't till after the shooting where Virge and Morg got hurt and the two McLowerys and Billy Clanton got killed that I learned all that led up to it. Lord knows we talked about it more than once over the years, and the way I see it, everything went back to that deal Wyatt made with Ike. Ike, being scared to death his gang would find out about the double-cross, somehow got the notion that Wyatt had told Doc about it. He hadn't—Wyatt was as close-mouthed as an Injun—but the night before the shooting Ike and Doc got into an argument. Ike started accusing Doc of telling everybody about the deal, and Doc, who didn't know what he was talking about, lost his temper—nothing un-usual about that—and told Ike to shut up and draw. Ike said he wasn't heeled, and damned fool that he was just kept on blabbing. Said to Doc that he'd played along with Wyatt just so he could lead him and his brothers into an ambush.

Doc, being Doc and half drunk, said: "You got your old man bumped off with your scheme."

Ike wanted to know what in hell Doc was talking about, and Doc said: "I pulled the trigger is how."

Up till then, nobody was sure it wasn't just Mexicans out there in Skeleton Cañon; probably Ike had thought so, too. But right then and there, Ike saw the light and swore he'd get even, said he'd be back the next day and Doc and the boys had better be waiting. Now Wyatt was listening to all this and would have liked to strangle Doc for letting the cat out of the bag, but there wasn't no taking it back. Besides, Wyatt finally figured Ike for the scum he was and knew he and Doc had to get the ring leaders of the Cowboy Gang before they got them. You see what I mean when I say it all was tangled up like a ball of yarn? It was double-dealing, politics, lying, killing, and Wyatt and Virge doing the best they could in a mess that nobody could've fixed. Everybody was hiding something or out for themselves, and there wasn't no way for us to win.

The morning after Ike and Doc had their fight, Ike was knocking on the door of Fly's Boarding House, looking for Doc, and he was carrying a Winchester and a pistol. He met Kate, and she came running down to the house. Virge was getting ready to leave when she came in panting for breath.

"Ike Clanton is looking for Doc. I told him Doc wasn't there. And when I told Doc about it, he . . . he got a look on his face that scared me. I'm afraid of what he's going to do."

Virge listened to her, and I watched him, knowing in my bones that something was up—like just before a thunderstorm when you can feel the lightning getting ready. That's how it was that morning.

Virge buckled on his pistol belt, looking serious. "Go on back, Kate. And stay inside. We'll handle it. God knows it's long overdue."

Then he left, me feeling limp as a rag doll and about as helpless.

Kate's eyes was wild. "We have to do something."

"What? Are you goin' after Ike yourself? Don't be stupid. Go on back to Fly's and wait it out." I didn't want her there. I didn't want anybody talking at me, making me more restless than I was.

"He could get killed."

"They all might." I spoke the truth, and hated hearing it, hated how my heart had started knocking in my chest.

When she was gone, I stood looking out my door at those cottonwoods that still had a few yellow leaves on 'em, and the Dragoons, sticking up like bare bones against the sky. A hawk flew over, its shadow quick and quiet, and I wrapped my arms around my middle and waited.

Ike wasn't making a secret of the fact that he was looking for a fight. He'd been mouthing off to everybody he came across, like the big blowhard that he was. Seems like half the town knew what he was after. When the boys went looking for him, they split up, and Morg and Virge found him. He made to point his Winchester at Virge, but Virge was too fast and grabbed it, and beat him over the head with his Colt. They took him over to Judge Wallace for a hearing, and Wyatt showed up. Even there Ike's mouth was going, threatening Morg and Wyatt till Wyatt got tired of hearing it. Can't say as I blame him. There comes a point when talk don't get it, and you just want the fight over and done with.

The way Wyatt told it, he called Ike a "damned, dirty cow thief" and said he'd be right if he shot him down for threatening his life and his brothers'. He said if Ike was so damned anxious to make a fight of it, he'd go anywhere on earth and do it, even over to the San Simon where the Cowboys hung out.

Ike, being who he was, said he'd see Wyatt after he was through in court. Said he only needed four feet of ground to fight on.

"I got up and left," Wyatt recalled. "I was so damned mad I might've drilled him right there. Outside, it wasn't any better. Tom McLowery was out there wantin' a fight, too. I told him to go after his Colt, but he claimed he wasn't heeled. So I buffaloed him and left him lyin' there. I went and got a cigar to cool off."

It wasn't long after that Wyatt saw Tom and Frank McLowery, Billy Clanton, and Ike in the gun shop, buying cartridges and stuffing 'em in their belts. Frank's horse was up on the sidewalk, and Wyatt went and put it back in the street, and, of course, Frank had to come out and get off some mouth.

About then, Wyatt met up with Virge, Morg, and Doc, and they was standing on the corner, talking about what to do, when Rube Coleman came along and said they'd better get down to the O.K. Corral and disarm Ike and the rest, 'cause they was looking to make trouble.

They headed over there and walked a ways down Frémont street and saw Behan down there, talking. After a minute, he walked away, looking back over his shoulder, but when he came up to the boys, he said he'd disarmed the bunch of 'em. That's just the kind of lie you'd expect from that snake in the grass, 'cause Frank's and Billy's pistols was in plain sight when the boys got down there.

The first thing Virge did was tell 'em to throw up their hands. Of course, they didn't. They went for their pistols, and Wyatt, who was wound up tighter than a spring and disgusted with all that'd been going on, decided to have it out there and then, and yelled: "You sons-of-bitches have been lookin' for a fight, and now you can have it!"

Virge yelled—"No, I don't want that!"—for all the good it did. No one was listening.

Not a minute later, there was three men dead or dying, Morg had got it across the back, and Virge in the leg. I heard the shots from where I was and went running, my skirts hitched to my knees, my only thought for Virge, my Virge, the other half of my heart.

I hadn't gone far when I damned near fell over Tom McLowery who was lying there propped against a wall, and I said: "Well, what son-of-a-bitch shot you?" It didn't make a lick of sense, but I was so addled I didn't know what I was saying. He wasn't in any shape to answer anyhow.

Out there on Frémont it was all dust and confusion—horses milling around, folks yelling, women screaming, but I picked out Wyatt, and then Virge. He was standing up, but had blood all over his pants leg. Morg was on his feet but looked pretty peaked. I went over and found out Virge was all right, then got Morg to sit down on the edge of a ditch that was running along there. Frank and Billy was being carried off, and I wondered where Ike was. Turned out, he'd run away during the fight, tried to grab Wyatt, and then took off like the yellow bugger he was.

Kate was there, holding onto Doc, her hair all sparkling with pieces of glass. She'd been watching the whole thing from Fly's, and a bullet had gone through the window right over her head. And then Sadie came hurrying up the street, her face chalk white, her hair flying around loose. She pushed and shoved till she was up close to Wyatt, and I saw her lips moving, saw him put a hand on her shoulder before turning away. Right then I knew how it was with the two of 'em, knew Mattie was doomed, and she knew it, too, 'cause she'd come up with Lou and Bessie and saw it like I did.

Jim had run up with a six-shooter in either hand when he heard the shooting start. He stuck 'em in his belt and went over to where Behan was jawing at Wyatt. Seemed the little crook wanted to arrest the Earps.

Wyatt brushed him off. "Not today," he said. "You tried to throw us off guard, sayin' you'd disarmed them, you little bastard."

Seeing as the crowd was listening, Behan had to get cocky. "I'm not one bit afraid of you," he said, looking up into Wyatt's face.

I was surprised Wyatt didn't knock him on his ass right there, but he didn't. All he said was: "I've been putting up with your bullshit too damn' long, Johnny." Then he walked away.

The vigilantes brought up a wagon and loaded Virge and Morg into it. They rolled it up to our place by hand, me running ahead. Thirty seconds, maybe a minute, and everything changed. All our hopes came crashing down that afternoon on that dusty street. It was October 26, 1881 in Tombstone, the town whose name stands for murder.

Chapter Thirty

That was an awful time! Virge and Morg healing up and griping like men do when they're helpless, the whole town taking sides till it wasn't safe to open the door unless you knew who was out there. Virge never took off his pistol, slept with it ready, and all of us went around jumpy, like we was on a hot stove, never knowing what to expect. And then Ike Clanton filed a murder charge against Wyatt and Doc, and that little scum, Behan, put 'em both in jail.

"They won't last a day before someone tries to off 'em," Jim said. "We oughta put a guard on the place."

John Clum had been thinking the same. He came down and told us not to worry, that the Citizen's Safety Committee was watching the jail day and night, which was kind of a relief but not much, knowing how useless they'd been in the past. Jim's comment on that was: "Hell, they're liable to shoot themselves instead of what they're aiming at if it comes to it."

Mattie came over to us and sat around, wringing her hands. "What's goin' to happen?" she kept saying. Her voice had got so small she sounded like a little girl.

For all that he was as worried as the rest, Virge was hopeful. "He'll be out in a day or two. There'll be a hearin', and he and Doc'll have to go, but if there's any right in this town, Wyatt and Doc will get off." Then he slapped his hand on his good leg. "Damn it all! I should be guardin' the jail, not that bunch of sissies!"

"You hush," I told him. "Don't fuss yourself, and don't go borrowin' trouble."

"He's my brother, damn it!"

"Don't I know."

Before we got into a shouting match, I went out to get some wood for the stove. The day had turned cold, the sky streaked with the hard, dark clouds of winter. Lord, I never felt as small, as helpless as I did standing out there all alone! I remember when, years later, Sadie said evil leaked like poison out of the ground. That day I could feel it curling around the house. And there wasn't any place where we'd be safe from it. Not there.

Virge had been right about one thing, though. Wyatt got out on bail, and Doc, too, and we was all having supper together when the knock came at the door.

Jim was sitting closest to it and got up, his hand on his pistol. When he looked out, whoever it was said—"I got the wrong house."—and turned and ran.

It took a minute to register, then Jim cussed. "God damn!" His eyes had that wolf look I'd seen in Wyatt's. "I thought there was something about that voice. That had to be that son-of-a-bitch Frank Stillwell dressed up like a damned woman!"

It would've been funny if things hadn't been like they was, and Wyatt banged his fist on the table. "That's the limit! We're moving to the Cosmopolitan. All of us. Down here we're sitting ducks for any of those bastards. Hell, they could take a shot through the window."

"Leave our homes?" I don't know why, but I figured we was safe in the house.

Wyatt leaned across the table, and those eyes of his went clear through me. "Yes, Allie. Leave or lose more than four walls and a roof. The next time they might plug Virge or Morg through a window, and this time it might not be in Virge's leg. Get that through your Irish head, you hear?"

It's the closest I ever heard him come to yelling at me, and Virge never said a word like he usually did when someone got on me. I heard all right. Turned out Wyatt's idea wasn't exactly new. Clum and some others in the Citizen's Safety Committee had been trying to talk Wyatt into moving us all to a hotel so they could help guard us. It was the first good sense I heard coming out of 'em, and for good reason. If Wyatt wasn't scared, they were. They didn't want to lose their protectors.

The next day we packed up and moved over to the hotel. I never thought to ask at the time who was paying the bill for that high-priced place. Thinking back, it had to be Wells Fargo and the Citizen's Committee the boys was working for. We couldn't have afforded it for long, but we sure lived like kings for the little while left to us, and I can't say I didn't like it, 'cause I did.

The hearing of the murder charge went on for almost a month in Judge Spicer's court. At first things looked bad. Ike Clanton lied through his teeth, saying that the boys had piped off some of the money that was in the strongbox on the Kinnear stage and had held it up to cover themselves. Said all he'd been doing that day of the shooting was protecting himself 'cause he was sure they was after him. But the biggest liar was Behan. He was a first-class liar. To hear him it sounded like a bunch of innocent little boys headed for Sunday school had been shot down. If I remember right, he said the Earp boys got off eight or ten shots before Frank had got his pistol out.

If I'd been in court, I'd've said: *Hell, if the Earp boys had got off eight or ten shots, Frank wouldn't have got his pistol out at all!* But I wasn't in court. Day after day I sat with Virge and Morg, Mattie, and Kate, and Lou, my hands shaking like cottonwood leaves, my heart beating so fast I thought I might die from it, wondering what would happen to us all if Wyatt got sent up on a murder charge. Would Virge and Morg be next, and, if they was, how long would any of 'em last in Behan's jail?

Virge and Morg, of course, wasn't down at court on account of being shot, so we all depended on Wyatt to come and tell us what was going on. And when he told us what Ike and Behan had said, told us the lies that had come out of 'em both, Virge blew up, so mad he liked to have split. "Law! What in hell kind of law is it with Behan perjurin' himself to get us swung off? What in hell kind of law is it that they listen to scum like Ike Clanton? Wait'll I get out of here and I'll see about this."

I was as mad as he was. Like him, I'd always believed in justice, and it came as a shock when justice and the law turned around and bit us. You never know when you hear about somebody else's bad luck, or read about it, what the real truth is. It was on account of Ike and Behan testifying first that Spicer had Wyatt and Doc jugged again, but a bunch of locals with money put up bail and got them out.

All that time Kate was sitting there, her hands clasped together so tight I could see the bones in 'em. She gave a laugh that sounded like the croak a raven makes. "Justice, justice! It's a dream! I saw how it worked in my own country and in Mexico, and this town, this dung heap, is worse! The devil lives here. Every place you look, in every face you see on the street is the devil. It sickens me. It all sickens me." She put her hands over her face, and her shoulders shook with her weeping.

We sat and stared at her. She was so different from all of us—a foreigner—but she'd put into words what all of us was thinking and feeling, and in that minute I loved her like I'd loved her in Deadwood. She was real and true and in spite of her differences one of us.

I been reading my so-called "life story" over again and can hardly believe what that fella wrote, but I know where he got it. He was reading the old lies that came out in *The Nugget* every day the hearing went on, and he believed all of it, the damned fool, not knowing *The Nugget* was Behan's newspaper and whatever was in there was nothing but a bunch of bullshit. I'm not gonna talk about it any more. It makes me too damned mad. But after all the testimony was in, Judge Spicer wrote that he didn't think a jury in Arizona Territory could be got up to convict the Earps or Doc on the evidence he'd heard. And to cap that, he said, if the grand jury that was sitting just then didn't agree, they was derned well welcome to bring a charge. They didn't.

I'll never forget one part of what he wrote because I thought he really had a way with words. It was about something Frank McLowery said when he was jawing with Behan down there before the shooting. He'd told Johnny Behan he'd give up his pistol if Johnny would disarm the Earps, too. And the damned fool Behan testified to it in court. Spicer wrote that for "desperate, reckless, and lawless men to demand that the chief of police and his assistants be disarmed is a proposition both monstrous and startling." Those words about summed it up all around. The whole affair in Tombstone fit that to a T.

Imagine those trouble-making sons-of-bitches thinking the police should be disarmed so they could stay in town and wait their chance!

I was for pulling out just as soon as Morg and Virge was in good enough shape to travel. So were all the rest of us women. You can imagine how far that got with a bunch of proud hardheads like the Earp boys. Virge spoke for all of 'em when he said: "I'll be ░░damned if I'll look like I'm running from that bunch."

If any of 'em had sense enough to leave, it was Jim, but he always went along with the other two. Not that he didn't have Earp guts. He was the one who'd run to the gunfight with two six-shooters ready to join the fuss.

Somehow, though, that crowd left him alone. I never figured why and neither did he. I asked him a time or two. He said: "Maybe because everybody knew I'd been crippled in the war. Besides, I never rode with those posses or got into an argument with any of 'em. Why should I? Wyatt and Virge handled that for me." Anyhow, he never felt like he had to move into the Cosmopolitan with the rest of us, and he was right. Nobody ever bothered him. Just as well for them. He'd've shot just as soon as his brothers. And he was a damned good shot, too.

After the hearing was over, we still stayed at the Cosmopolitan to look out for Morg. I suppose if things had blown over, we'd have moved back down to First and Frémont, but things didn't blow over. Pretty soon Judge Spicer started getting death threats in the mail. Then somebody tried to kill John Clum. He was on his way out of town on the stage, headed back East to be with his kid for Christmas. They tried to make it look like another stage hold-up and pulled it off one dark night just like when they had their shot at Bob Paul. They shot a horse, and hit the driver in the leg, and that stopped the coach. Then some damned fool yelled—"Get the old bald-headed son-of-a-bitch!"—which sure as hell gave them away. John was bald as a peeled egg. He wasn't no fool and jumped out in the dark, and hid, then walked down to the Grand Central Mill in Contention and communicated the news to Wyatt.

"Clum should 'a' expected it," Virge said. "He's in it as deep as we are."

"Ain't it ever gonna be over?" I asked.

He shook his head. "Not till every one of the bastards is run out or dead."

"Better hope it's them and not us," I said, 'cause I had a hunch something else bad was gonna happen.

Well, it did.

The first I knew, they was helping Virge up to our room—Wyatt, Doc Goodfellow, and a couple of other docs. Virge could barely walk and was close to fainting with blood running all down one side. They got him in bed as easy as they could, but more like a sack of potatoes, me fussing around trying to help and getting in the way.

"Is he dyin'?" I could hardly get the words out because I was crying so hard and had a big lump in my throat, wondering what I'd ever do without him.

He opened his eyes then and looked at me, said: "Not by a damned jug full. And I still got one good arm to hug you with."

I cried all the harder at that—him next to death's door just thinking about loving me and trying to make me feel better.

Goodfellow got Virge's clothes off and took a look at his left arm. I damned near fainted at the sight. It was practically shot off at the elbow. By then Chris Billicke who owned the place had some more lamps brought in so there was light enough for the docs to get to work. They gave Virge some shots of dope and got the bleeding mostly stopped.

The operation seemed to me to take forever, and I've got the memory in my head—the light of the lamps, the docs, their sleeves rolled up, bent over Virge, taking out a bunch of splintered bone, and always the blood, the rags soaked with it, the smell of it like metal in my mouth. Nobody can know unless they've lived it how it feels watching such a thing and worrying what to do if or when the man you love wakes up. I got a big lift when Doc Goodfellow, who was always a friend to the Earps, said: "Missus Earp, I'm going to stay here tonight if you don't mind."

"Mind?" I almost kissed the man.

He sent George Parsons to get him some things at his office up the street. I didn't know George yet then, except I knew he was in the Citizen's Safety Committee and a friend of Clum's. I used to see a lot of him and Clum when Wyatt was still alive and they'd come to visit. Once they even brought Tom Mix who wanted to meet me. But that's getting away from my story.

By then Morg was up and walking, and he came in and looked at Virge, who was lying there with his eyes shut and his face white. "Allie," he said, and give me a hug that made me feel just a mite better. Then he looked at Wyatt. Neither of 'em said a word. Didn't have to. That look said it all.

Wyatt got warrants sworn out for Ike and his brother Phinn, and Curly Bill, who witnesses said were the ones did the shooting. They even found a hat of Ike's over where the bastards had been waiting for one of the Earps to come out of the Oriental. Wyatt took posses out, and inside a week Morg was riding with him. The Earps was tough. The Clantons was all yellow and came in and gave themselves up, 'cause they didn't want to run across Wyatt away out in the country somewhere. Of course, they had alibis and was turned loose. I was always sorry Wyatt didn't run across them out in the sticks. It wouldn't have fixed up Virge, but I'd have felt a damned sight better knowing they was coyote bait.

We had a room down at the front of the hall, and Clum had a man there twenty-four hours a day, and Wyatt or Morg or some of their friends was there, too, when they were in town. Wyatt had got appointed U.S. deputy marshal in Virge's place, and he had a bunch of tough deputies like Doc, Turkey Creek Jack Johnson, Texas Jack Vermillion, and Sherm McMasters working for him. About then Warren came back, too. He was an Earp, whatever else you say about him, and he had guts like the rest. Come to think of it, that's what got him killed over in Willcox some years later. That, and he didn't have a lick of sense.

I hardly slept for a couple of days, but they brought in a cot so I could be right there in case Virge needed something. I used to sit there with the lamp low at night and watch him breathing and pray he'd take another breath, and another, and try to make my strength go into his body. Pray? I must have worn a tunnel straight up to heaven for a month, and all the while I was praying, too, that after this maybe he'd have the sense to leave. There wasn't one of us women who didn't talk about leaving. It felt like we didn't have a real life at all, just worries about which of our men would be next.

Lou had it in her head that she and Morg should go back to Colton, or even up to Montana, but Morg wasn't having any of that. "Can't he see?" she asked one day. "Can't any of 'em see it's hopeless stayin' here?"

"It ain't their way to pull out," I said, knowing how the boys was made.

"And it ain't in Wyatt to leave that woman. We could all

get shot for all he cares." Mattie, in those days, was falling apart in front of our eyes, and nothing we could do to help.

She was dead right, but I couldn't say so, and said instead: "We don't know that's what's keepin' him here."

She gave me a look of pure hate. "You'd stick up for the devil."

"And that ain't true, either." I felt like shaking her.

"Don't let us fight." Lou came and stood between us. "It's bad enough without that."

Of course, she was right. She usually was. Even now there's times when I wish I could hear her laughing, or watch her talking to her flowers as if they could hear her. Maybe they did. It ain't in me to say.

It wasn't long after Ike Clanton was cleared of attempting to kill Virge that he filed another murder charge against Wyatt, Morg, and Doc. Behan probably put him up to it. The J.P. down at Contention swore out a warrant on Ike's complaint and Behan pulled the three of 'em in and was planning to take them down there in a wagon. And he did that all right, but it didn't work out like he expected.

When he was all set to go, a big posse from the Citizen's Safety Committee showed up. Johnny, of course, got all mouthy and asked 'em what the hell they thought they was doing. Colonel Herring, who was one of Wyatt's lawyers that got him off at the hearing, was in charge of the posse, and said: "Why, Johnny, we thought we'd come along for a little air."

There must have been thirty men in his posse out for that airing. Wyatt said later: "That little J.P. took one look at Herring's crowd, all hung down with guns, and decided he didn't have jurisdiction."

Back in Tombstone, Herring got a writ of *habeas corpus* from Judge Lucas, so they was free again. It was the last time that snake Behan tried to get them in court or in his jail where everyone knew he'd let someone shoot them.

The end of our Tombstone years came, but in a way that tore us apart and broke our hearts, Lou's most of all. She got her wish to go back to Colton, but she sure didn't want to go as a widow.

It was March, the night before Wyatt's birthday, and Virge and I was in our room, planning a small celebration, when Warren busted in without knocking, his face twisted like something inside him was broke.

"They shot Morg," he said.

"Bad?" Virge looked like he'd been shot again.

Warren wasn't one to mince words. "He's dyin'."

The first thing I thought was to go to Lou, then I remembered she had a brother over at Dos Cabezas and was visiting him. The thought went through my mind: *Poor Lou. This'll just about kill her.*

Virge said: "Where did it happen?"

"Down at Bob Hatch's. They got him layin' on a couch down there."

Bob Hatch's was a saloon and pool hall just up the street.

Virge said: "Help me up, you two. I wanna see him before he goes. Are you sure he's a goner?"

"Doc Goodfellow thinks so."

My heart sank right there, and I started crying. "I'm comin' with you," I said. I expected Virge to have something to say about me coming into a saloon, but he didn't. Maybe he didn't even hear me.

When we got there, Morg was still alive. He opened his eyes when Virge took his hand, and tried to smile. Virge was crying, and who could blame him? I wanted to kiss Morg for Lou—and for myself for that matter—before he went, and I should have, but his brothers was all around him. I wish I'd shoved them out of the way.

Morg motioned Wyatt down and whispered something to him. Wyatt never would say what. I was holding back my own tears, and must've made a noise, 'cause Morg looked at me like he was trying to say something, but it was too late. He just shut his eyes and stopped breathing. He'd been shot in the back while he was playing pool. That's how those bastards operated. They didn't have guts enough to face the boys fair.

We got Virge back to our room, and he flopped onto the bed and put his good arm over his face. I thought maybe he was dying, knowing how close the boys was. But after a minute he said: "The damned, dirty back-shooters! Morg didn't deserve to go like that. If it wasn't for this damn' arm, I'd be out there lookin' for 'em."

Finally he fell asleep with his clothes still on, and I put the blankets over him careful so as not to wake him. I don't think I slept at all that night, worrying all over again, and thinking about Lou.

I didn't see Wyatt again until morning when he came to our room. He was a sight—looked like he hadn't slept, either. Morg and him had been kids together on the farm, and Wyatt always thought he had to take care of him.

"I'm goin' after those bastards wherever I can find them," he said to Virge, sounding like he was talking to himself. And that's what he did.

It was a hell of a birthday present, I thought, feeling bad for him, and for us all.

The next day they had a coroner's jury hearing, and Pete Spence's wife testified that her husband and Frank Stillwell and some others had been the ones. The boys knew the other names, but I didn't and still don't, but I know who

Wyatt made pay for it. Pete Spence, like a damned fool, had told his wife to keep her mouth shut about what she knew and then beat her and her mother who lived with them to make sure she did. What he made sure of was that she talked. She had Mexican and Injun blood mixed and didn't take to getting whipped, or having her ma beat. He should have known that. All of those Cowboys was dumb, like I said, and mean, not caring for anybody but their own selves.

After the coroner's hearing, we pulled out, taking Morg's body back to the old folks in Colton to bury him. Us women had a time with Lou, who hadn't stopped crying since she'd come back and found her husband shot in the back. Morg was all she had, all she'd ever wanted, and there was nothing we could say or do to bring him back.

We went by wagon to catch the train at Contention, and a bunch of the Cowboy Gang trailed after us, staying out of rifle range, the bastards! They was still determined to get even before the Earps got out of their territory. But we had our own bunch guarding us—friends of the boys who was riding alongside, and I was wearing a new black coat with Virge's pistol strapped on underneath where he could grab it with his good hand. I wish I'd taken a shot at some of those men following us. I'd have loved to see one bite the dust.

Well, one of 'em did at Tucson where the train stopped to let the passengers off to eat. Wyatt, Warren, and Doc came in the restaurant with us, and, while we was eating, a deputy U.S. marshal came over and told Wyatt that some of the Gang was in town and to expect trouble. After we was finished, they took us back to the train, then went outside to check around.

That's when a shot came right through the train window,

close enough for us to feel it passing. Virge shoved me down, then grabbed his pistol.

Outside, Wyatt and Doc saw Frank Stillwell running off, and followed. They wasn't sure who it was, but it looked like he was headed to where he could take another shot at the train when it pulled out. When they got close enough to see, Wyatt let him have it with both barrels of his shotgun, and Doc sieved him with his six-shooter. Doc had taken Morg's death nearly as hard as the Earp brothers. I heard later that he'd gone through Tombstone the night of the shooting, kicking in doors and ready to kill the first one of the murderers he found.

When our train pulled out, Wyatt and Doc went back to Tombstone and from there on a killing spree. Within a week Wyatt killed not only Stillwell, but a feller named Indian Charlie that was up to his neck in it, and Curly Bill. Then he blew the country to let things cool down. The next summer he was back and got Ringo. What a reunion that bunch must have had in hell.

Behan and his cronies wanted to bring Wyatt and Doc back from Colorado where they went after Tombstone, to try them for getting Stillwell, but couldn't swing it. The governor of Colorado was onto their game, and, besides, he was friends with Wyatt and Doc.

And that's how our big plans to make a fortune ended. But us Earps knew how to make do, and we had to often enough. The boys was all drifters, and, as they say, "a rolling stone gathers no moss." We gathered a little every once in a while, but never seemed to be able to hang onto it.

I've lived a long while since Tombstone and a lot of things happened, some of 'em pretty exciting, which I'll get to. Mostly, though, what I wanted to tell was about Virge and me and the truth about Tombstone. As I heard the boys say many times: "We was just lawmen and had a job to do." And they did it damned well, and not a one of them was crooks, except maybe Warren, who had a mean streak and, being the youngest boy, was probably spoiled. But the kind we had to deal with around Tombstone made Warren look like an angel with wings.

Chapter Thirty-One

We was a sorry bunch on the train. Somehow word got out who we were, and people either avoided us or tried to sympathize. The conductor got us a seat away from the broken window. While we was pulling out, Wyatt run up alongside the window and held up one finger, and yelled: "I got number one for Morg!"

Over the years when him and Virge talked about it, Wyatt always said: "I should 'a' got number one for Morg before they got him."

He was a different man after Tombstone. Talked even less than he had before and had spells when he seemed like he wasn't there. He reminded me of the men I'd seen coming home from the war, men with a haunted look in their eyes and a way of carrying themselves that kept folks from getting too close.

Virge was different, too, for that matter, but he hadn't done the killing, and that bothered him. He kept saying: "I'm gonna go back and help Wyatt clean out that bunch." But, of course, he didn't—couldn't with his arm damned near useless. He never got over that, either, although, being Virge, he tried not to let it show.

We was all changed after Tombstone. It does something to you to know that the world doesn't really give a damn for justice until injustice hits so close to home. We went there as innocent and hopeful as kids, and came out old—and maybe the wiser for it—but I reckon I'd have rather stayed a kid.

We was a sorry bunch all right, but nothing compared to Morg's folks who met us at the train. We'd wired ahead, of course, and they knew what had happened. They was all there, waiting, Ma, looking like she hadn't slept in a week, and Pa, grieving but trying to be strong for her sake. But that old woman was tough as oak wood. If she cried for Morg, she did it where nobody could see, and at the station her concern was all for Lou who she pulled into her arms.

"My daughter," she said. "My poor daughter," and Lou leaned into her trembling, her tears falling like rain.

Adelia and Bill was there, too, and I was glad to see 'em again, but how I wished we could've got together at a happier time. We hugged each other, and Adelia hugged Virge, careful of his arm that was still strapped up.

We probably would've stood there, all holding onto each other for a long time, but Pa came over to Virge and put a hand on his shoulder and said: "Come on, Son. Let's get home." His voice cracked, and I saw he was hurting for his boys—the one in the box, and the one crippled, and Wyatt out there facing the killers alone.

The day we buried Morg was one of them misty southern California spring days, not cold but dismal, with low-hanging clouds and showers that fell on us every once in a while. Mount Slover, all bare white rock, hung over us and gave me shivers, looking like it was going to fall over and bury us, too. It's mostly gone now. Somebody found out it was good for making cement and started tearing it down a little every year.

That cemetery's gone now. The railroad changed its

main line to run through there, and all the bodies got moved to another cemetery. I wasn't in town when that happened, but Adelia told me that a handle broke off Morg's coffin, and the men carrying it dropped it. When I heard that, I thought that bad luck followed poor Morg even to the grave and beyond.

Speaking of beyond, I hope he's where he deserved to go. If he is, if there is such a place, I bet he never run into any of the crowd that killed him—or that double-dealing Behan, either.

Back at the house after the funeral, Ma gave Lou something to drink that put her to sleep. When we'd got her in bed, I remember Ma brushing the hair off Lou's forehead, as gentle as if she was touching a baby bird.

"She's wore out, poor thing. She never had anything but heart, and that's broke," Ma said.

"We're all broke." I knew that to be true.

She shook her head. "Not you, though you might think it. And not me. I've buried more than one child, and it hurts worse'n anything to do it. But you go on. There ain't anything else you can do with the living ones still in need of you."

There she stood, like a little black sparrow in her funeral dress, giving me a piece of herself. I never loved anybody more than I loved her in that minute. She gave me a pat. "Now, come on. We'll get the food on the table. Folks are always hungry after a buryin'."

I followed her to the kitchen, thinking she must've been up all night cooking, and that maybe that was how she dealt with grieving. By then, Bessie and Jim and Mattie had come. They'd stayed behind in Tombstone packing up things, so there was a crowd at the table, a sad, quiet crowd. We was the survivors, if that's what we could be called—survivors, and changed for always.

We stayed with the old folks for a while, but it was pretty crowded with Mattie and Lou there, so we went and moved in with Adelia and Bill Edwards up at Yucaipa. Bill was farming and raising bees. They called him "The Bee King", and it was a treat watching him work around the hives, the bees all in a swarm but never stinging him. He had the touch, like Ma Earp had, for living things.

Little Ginnie Ann, named after Ma Earp, had been born in 1880, and nothing would do but that Virge had to hold her and sing her songs I'd never heard him sing. He was always crazy about kids, especially Adelia's. Later on he wanted to adopt her daughter, Estelle, but Adelia said she couldn't spare a one of 'em. There's times now I wish I hadn't been so damned smart and we'd had kids of our own. But I could never see dragging a kid around with us, the kind of life we led. Maybe I was wrong, but it's too late to take it back.

Virge was getting stronger every day, but his arm was pretty useless. In May we went to San Francisco to have it looked at by what we hoped was better doctors, although Doc Goodfellow was as good as any. Wells Fargo footed the bill. I guess they was looking out for us all.

A clipping from the Prescott *Courier* of May 27, 1882 that I kept all these years tells how we was doing in Virge's own words. Reading it over, I can hear his voice yet.

LETTER FROM VIRGIL EARP

James M. Dodson, our city marshal, yesterday received the following letter from V.W. Earp:

Colton, California, May 22, 1882.

FRIEND JIM:—thinking you would like to hear

from me, I will drop you a few lines. I am here trying to get well. My back is nearly well; my arm is about healed up, but will never be very useful. I was shot in the elbow and it was unjointed and six inches of bone taken out upwards. I can use my hand as good as ever, but the arm will never be limber. Of course, you have heard of our trouble. It was simply caused by doing our duty as officers. Wyatt and Warren Earp have not been arrested, but Doc Holliday was [arrested] at Denver, I understand. They got him out on *habeas corpus*. The Earps will stand trial when court meets, would surrender now if they would give bail. I often hear of you, and I see you handle the roughs after my style, but you have a different community there from what I had in Tombstone. When you have trouble, they say, Go it, Jim, we will back you.

I will start for San Francisco day after tomorrow to get my arm looked at, may stay twenty days. If you write as soon as you receive this, direct it to 169 Market Street, San Francisco. As soon as I come back, I will go back to Tombstone. I would like to hear from you as soon as possible, and by all means give my regards to all Prescott folks. It is the only place that seems like home.

I remain your true friend and well-wisher.

VIRGIL W. EARP

I couldn't have said it better, about what seemed like home. We should never have left Prescott, and after we left Frisco—with the bad news that Virge wouldn't ever get the full use of his arm—we talked about going back there.

Both of us was upset over what the doctors had said. We had some hard days for a while, mostly wrangling over what we was going to do, how we was going to live. Virge had the bone-headed idea that he'd go back to Tombstone and even up some scores, but finally it was clear enough even for an Earp to see what Behan had in mind if he went back. He'd have to kill and run like Wyatt did. If he didn't, he'd end up in Behan's jug, a short stay for Johnny's friends and a one way trip for his enemies. There wasn't an honest bone in that man, or a decent one, either.

Doc had put it pretty well in a newspaper interview in Denver when he said: "Doc Holliday is a goner if he goes back there." When I read that, I said to Virge: "He's got more sense than you do. He'd like to live a while yet."

Virge's trouble was he didn't like loose ends and hated being crippled while Wyatt did his fighting for him. "I oughta be out there instead of sitting here feeling worthless."

I got mad as hell when he said that. I lost my temper a lot in those days. "You ain't worthless. Not to me, not to anybody else. And if you think I'll let you go stick your head in a noose, you're plain foolish! I'll damn' well tie you to the bedpost if you try!"

He laughed his old laugh that cheered me a little. "I'd like to see you try!"

"Just watch me!"

He never did go back, and in July came word that Wyatt and Doc had been spotted in that country. And then John Ringo was found dead—stuck up in a tree on the side of a road. The coroner's jury called it "suicide", but we knew better. There wasn't no powder burns on his head where he was supposed to have shot himself.

I never asked Wyatt about it. He wouldn't have told me anyhow, but I suspect he told Virge, who kept it to himself. It was about then that Wyatt loaned us some money, and I guessed where he got it. But he never said anything, and never expected it back. He was good that way—and maybe he felt a little guilty on account of what happened.

While all this was going on, there was trouble in Colton. Mattie was driving Ma and Pa Earp crazy with her whining and fussing. It was—"When's Wyatt comin' for me?"—and—"I might as well be widowed like Lou."—day and night till Ma got tired hearing it.

She sat Mattie down and told her to behave, and, if she ever said that about being a widow in front of Lou again, why she'd slap her bald-headed. After that there was peace for a while, but I think everybody except Mattie knew Wyatt wasn't coming for her. He had friends sneak Sadie out in a buggy after we left, and she was back in San Francisco waiting for him.

I don't know who I felt sorrier for—Lou, sickly and mourning Morg, or Mattie, who never really had a chance. Eventually she pulled out and went back to Tombstone.

She came to see me just before she left, stood there looking like a kid that's been abandoned. "I come to say good bye," she said. "He's never written me as much as a line. Not one. I reckon he's never coming back. He's going to her, and so I'm leaving."

It came to me that as brave as Wyatt was facing the McLowerys and the Clantons, and anybody else that was after him, he was a damned coward when it came to telling the woman he'd been with for ten years he was through. I suppose he thought that saying it would only make things worse. I know he did send her money every once in a while till she died, but that was only when he was flush. I didn't say what I was thinking, only: "I'm sorry. We was sisters a while, and I reckon we'll always be. What'll you do?"

Her mouth drooped, and her shoulders. She looked like

a flower that was dying for lack of attention. "Go back to work."

"Child . . . ," I started, then stopped, knowing there was nothing I could do or say to make it right. She didn't know how to do anything else.

"I'll make out."

"You write if you don't."

"Lovin' somebody ain't always enough, is it?"

Well, it's not. Love never kept a one of us from hurt, or heartbreak, or death. "It ain't never all there is," I told her, then hugged her tight. "You take care."

Her eyes was blank like she was already gone. "What for?"

"I told you once. For yourself. A little pride don't hurt." I hugged her again, and she was gone.

I heard she lived in the Tombstone house a while, then went up to Globe. Kate took her in, and it says a lot for Kate that she treated Mattie damned good, considering, but in the end Mattie went back to whoring. Whether it was that, or that she never could forgive Wyatt, I don't know, but she finally committed suicide. I heard it was too much laudanum and booze, and I believe it, knowing her like I did.

Lou left, too. Took a job house cleaning in Los Angeles, although how she did it, having no strength, is a puzzle. She got remarried, but didn't last long after that. Reckon she died of grieving for Morg, being the kind who loves only once. I can understand that. And right here I'm saying good bye to Tombstone and everything about it. We never did go back there, thank the Lord. I only passed by on the train, a few times with Virge and once after he died. There was never a man like him, at least not that I ever saw. We was together for thirty-one years, and for all the trouble I can say I'd do it again in a minute just to be with him and hear him laugh.

Chapter Thirty-Two

The years just got away too fast after that. We had a lot of good times, for the most part, but, looking back, I can see that marrying a man with an itchy foot never gave me what I thought I wanted. Oh, I had love aplenty. There was never any doubt of that. But a woman likes a home. All gals want to make a nest.

Well, I know LaVonne has to leave in a few days, so I'm just gonna hit the high spots from here on out. Mostly I wanted to straighten out the lies told about Tombstone, and I reckon I got that done. It was exactly the way I told it.

It wasn't long after Mattie took off that Wyatt showed up in Colton with Sadie. I always wondered how she felt, meeting the family for the first time and knowing she'd taken Mattie's place. She didn't show no signs of being embarrassed, though, just acted a little quiet and shy, and said she hoped she wasn't putting anybody to any trouble on her account.

Being me, I said the first thing that came to mind which was: "I'm just glad you got rid of that little wife-beatin' bastard before it was your turn."

She laughed at that, sounded like a little bird singing up in a tree, and said: "Me, too, Allie. Oh, me, too. And I'm so happy with Wyatt."

As far as that goes, Wyatt was happier than I'd ever seen him. It would've been easy to blame him for deserting Mattie, but, watching him and Sadie, I couldn't hold that against him. He'd found the woman who was made for him, and that was the end of it.

The rest of the family felt like I did, and, when Adelia's daughter was born, she named her after Sadie—Estelle Josephine Edwards. Estelle grew up and married Bill Miller, and it's their daughter, LaVonne, I'm telling this to. I stayed close to 'em all these years, don't know how I'd have made it otherwise. It ain't easy being old and poor, but having a family like them helps a lot. Sometimes I stay with Estelle and Bill, and he obliges me by singing my favorite song every night. It's "Stay in Your Own Backyard", and he sings it real well. Usually he'll dance me around like I'm sixteen, and tease me when my skirt flies up and everybody sees the snuff can tucked in the top of my stocking.

There I go, rambling again. Lord it's hard keeping the years straight. There's so many of 'em, and they was all so long ago.

We stayed on in Colton for a few years. Virge ran for city constable and got elected, and, when Colton decided to make itself a real city, he was elected city marshal. I was so damned proud of him I nearly split! Best of all was when Wells Fargo gave him a gold marshal's badge for all he'd done for 'em in Tombstone.

"Let Johnny Behan chew on that!" was what I said, admiring how that badge shone on his coat. "Nobody's ever goin' to give him an eighty-dollar gold badge."

"Or ever will. If we're lucky, somebody'll give him a pine box."

Every time I thought of that man, which I tried hard not to do, I got a stomachache like I took poison, and Virge knew it. He grabbed me around the waist with his good arm. "Forget him. We're goin' out to celebrate."

We did, too, and, while we was having dinner, it seemed like half the town came up to congratulate him, me sitting there grinning like a monkey, I was so happy for him. That was a good time for us. Virge was getting paid regular, and, when he got reëlected, he bought me a house—put right in the deed it was 'cause he loved me and 'cause I'd stuck with him in Tombstone when he was near dying.

When he showed me what he'd gone and done, I sat down and bawled, couldn't stop, and there he was hopping around wondering why I was crying. Well, it was 'cause I'd never expected such a thing, never thought he'd put in writing what he felt.

"What did I do?" he kept asking, until I got to seeing how funny it was, me crying on one of the best days of my life. And when I told him, he shook his head, mumbling something about never understanding women. Well, I don't always understand 'em myself, come to it. What I do know is that bad news often comes on the heels of good.

It was about that time that Jim came one night with the word that Bessie was dying. She'd not been well for some time, and my first thought was: *There's another of us gone.*

I went over to her quick as I could and, seeing her, got a shock. She was pale as the sheet she was lying on, and coughing just like I'd heard Doc cough.

"Take care of Jim," she said when she could talk, and I said: "Jim don't need takin' care of."

"That's what you think." It was a whisper. Then she laid her head on the pillow and shut her eyes.

When the burying was over, I said to Virge: "I'd hoped we was done with funerals for a while."

"You and me will outlive 'em all," he said.

He was half right. I'm still here, and it's damned lonesome. All this telling of it makes it worse, but I'm near done with the telling, and with living, too, and glad of it. Experience should've told me we wouldn't keep that house in Colton for long. We didn't. Virge was running boxing matches all over those parts, and gambling, and he and Wyatt had got interested in racing again. I think it was in the late summer of 1890 that we moved to San Luis Obispo where Virge was following the horses. There I was looking at the ocean, and thinking back about how Lou was always collecting shells and stones and such. I started my own collection, kept it in an old wood box, and carried that box with me all over, 'cause you can bet we moved again and again over the next years. I got used to living out of a trunk and always having to leave something behind. That's what finally happened to my sewing machine that I'd held onto for years. It got left somewhere, I can't remember where now, and for a long time I felt like a piece of me was missing, I was so used to sitting at it making curtains and things.

Horses, boxing, gambling, and saloons kept Wyatt and Virge—and Sadie and me—on the move. We was back in San Bernardino when Ma Earp got sick and took to her bed. None of us ever expected she was gonna die on us. She had too much to live for—all the things she was always taking care of, her little birds with maybe a broken wing, or starving kitties that always seemed to know where to wander in, or pups—and, of course, her Nick, who she always called Mister Earp.

I was there to see her every day and wait on her if she wanted any little thing, and so was Virge. I never thought she was going to give out, but Pa Earp was worried, although he wasn't the type to show it. Then one night there was a knock on our door. I knew what it had to be. Pa had called the doctor, and then, when they knew Ma was sinking fast, he sent a neighbor kid over to get me and Virge. She was gone before we got there.

When I saw her laying dead with her arms folded, like they always did, I knew they'd put silver dollars on her eyelids because, by the time we got there, she looked like she was just sleeping, since they took the dollars off when they was sure her eyes would stay shut. Funny I thought of that, and remember it yet.

The doctor was still there. "Pneumonia," he said. "It's what most folks her age die from."

Pa was sitting beside the bed, still as I'd ever seen him except for making fists of his hands. I knew he'd like to cry. I went over and put my arms on his shoulders and he let out a big sigh.

"I always thought I'd go first, and worried about how she'd get along without me." He was quiet a long while, then said: "Now I gotta figure out how to get along without her. It's been over fifty years, and we come a long ways together."

I was crying by then. I wondered the same thing. She'd always been there for all of us.

Virge was out in the sitting room in a chair. He didn't want his pa to see him crying and maybe break down himself. I'd only seen Virge break down once before when Morg had gone. I cried with him, wishing I'd told her I'd loved her and how she'd given all of us some of her strength. Thinking about that, I figured maybe she hadn't kept nothing back, had plumb wore herself out giving to folks.

Virge said: "Somehow I never figured on her dyin'."

It makes no difference how old you are. Losing a

mother's always a shock. You find out that you're on your own, no matter if you're fifty or twelve like I was.

"She was the best Ma ever," I said, trying to comfort him. "Just be glad you had her long as you did. What'll happen to Pa?"

He kind of smiled at that. "He'll make out. He always does."

It was January and cold and nasty when we had the funeral. Wyatt and Jim was out on the desert somewhere and Sadie was home in San Francisco, so we never got word to them in time. When they started to throw the clods onto the coffin after it was all over, I said a prayer for her. It was a better one than the minister said, too—short and sweet. I remembered what the Mexicans always said: *"Vaya con Dios."* She always had, anyhow.

I took care of the last of her animals and birds and found homes for them, or turned loose the wild ones when they was well, and I was glad I could do that for her. I wondered if she was a-looking down, watching me and helping me figure out how to do everything. She must have been because I didn't know much about the wild ones. They seemed to know Ma was gone and looked for her, but they took to me, too—maybe her spirit was there, telling 'em to.

We buried Ma near Morg on another cold and rainy day, all of us still trying to make sense out of life without her in it. Adelia stood there with a little row of her kids beside her, looking mighty sad. They knew the sun had gone out of their life, because their grandma had petted every one of 'em. The rain was dripping off Adelia's hat onto her face so you couldn't tell which was rain and which was tears. She looked like a little kid herself—one who'd lost everything.

"It won't be the same," she said to me. "Life won't be the same without her in it."

There wasn't anything I could say to comfort her, knowing too well what she meant. I just put my arm around her and pulled her close, and we held onto each other like the orphans we'd become with Ma's passing.

Sure enough, Nick Earp got married again not three years later, and to a gal who could've been his daughter. Must've been something in the Earp blood that kept 'em going.

It was right after Ma died when Virge got the idea to head for a new gold strike at Vanderbilt. Word had it that there was so much gold everybody would soon be rich as that big bug back East, so they named the town for him. Virge got a wagon and piled it with lumber and nails, and there wasn't room for much more than the two of us and the clothes we was wearing by the time he got done loading. We took one of his boxers with us to handle the heavy work. Virge couldn't throw a harness on a team any more. The boxer was a nice young fellow named Flynn, who I remember was always laughing and joking. He called Virge "Grandpa," after he got to know him well enough to be sure Virge wouldn't plug him. All it got out of Virge was a grin. He was fifty and could have been somebody's grandpa— maybe he was already, 'cause he had a daughter, as I was gonna find out soon enough. I don't remember if her son, George, was born yet then. Later Flynn got to be a pretty good professional boxer, but by then we lost track of him except in the papers.

I'll tell you when I got my first look at that place I wanted to turn around and go right back to Colton. There was mountains and desert, and not much else but the mess that makes up any mining camp—shacks, tents, machinery, garbage, piles of rock, and mine tailings just scattered all over like a twister had dumped on the place and moved on.

I thought of Pa Earp's little orange grove, and Ma's tidy kitchen with always a critter or two hanging around the door—I couldn't get used to the fact she wasn't there—and said to Virge: "This is as close to hell as I want to get."

It was worse than that. In summer the heat burned us right through our clothes, and there wasn't any water at first. It had to be carted in across the desert, and it made keeping clean a chore. I got so I felt like one of those lizards that crawled everywhere, all dusty and dried up and tired of it all.

Virge built himself a big two-story saloon and was soon making money with gambling and putting on boxing matches upstairs. After that was done, he built us a little house out of rock, and I got busy making it into a home. Except I wanted a sewing machine for curtains and such, and asked Virge if we could send for one.

"It'll just be something else to leave behind when we go," was his answer.

I wasn't used to him telling me no. Besides, I'd had enough of sitting around doing nothing but wait for him to come home, and told him so. Loud. Probably they heard me down in some of the mine shafts.

Virge didn't say a word back, just turned and left me there, fuming. He never came home that night, and I was fuming even worse by morning when an Injun came to the door. He was hungry and wearing just enough to keep him decent. I gave him a cup of coffee, and that's when the idea came to me.

It wasn't right, him walking around like that, and there was Virge's fancy dress suit hanging all alone on its hook. And me, seeking revenge.

"Here," I said, holding out the coat and pants. "You take 'em."

He didn't wait. Just grabbed that suit and put it on, leaving me feeling good for the first time since Virge'd left.

Oh, he was mad as fire when he got home and found out what I'd done! But I stood my ground. Told him just how I felt, him gone all the time, and me sitting home about as useful as a stick. Thinking I'd shame Virge, I even brought up Wyatt, and how he'd got my first machine to Tombstone when everybody else had said there wasn't no room.

"You get me a sewin' machine," I told him. "It's the least you can do. And I'll make you another suit first off. But I don't like it here. I don't like doin' nothin' all day. And the sooner we leave, the happier we'll both be."

It wasn't long till the machine came in on a freight wagon, and I got busy making Virge a nice, new suit. Not long after that, the strike started playing out, like most did sooner or later, and we pulled out, taking my sewing machine with us. Can't say I ever missed that town. It ain't worth remembering except for the sight of that Injun hopping into those black pants that was too long for him, then strutting down the street proud as hell of himself.

After that it was Cripple Creek, Oklahoma for the land run, and the Texas Panhandle where we thought we might settle and get a ranch. But in the end we went back to Arizona, and that's where Virge nearly got himself killed a third time.

Chapter Thirty-Three

When they carried Virge in, he was lying so still and looked so bad, his face bloody and the wound in his head still bleeding, I was sure he was dead. My feet felt like they was froze to the floor, and I swear my heart stopped beating, 'cause without him life wasn't worth much. Seems the mine he'd been working out in Hassayampa had caved in, and he'd got caught and buried under rocks and timber.

The doctor put an arm around me to hold me up. "He's alive, Missus Earp. Unconscious, but alive."

"He's hurt bad." It came out scratchy, my mouth had gone so dry.

"I think he'll make it."

I got hold of myself, knowing Virge would need all the strength I had and then some. "What can I do?"

The doc—I think his name was Abbott—patted my shoulder. "Get me some warm water and clean rags. While he's out, I'm going to relocate his hip and shoulder and clean him up. Then we'll see."

We saw, all right. I still don't know how Virge made it. His feet was crushed, his legs was swelled and turning blue, and the cut on his head looked like it'd gone clear through and smashed the bone. I couldn't let myself think. Just turned into a pair of hands doing what the doc said—

picking bits of rock and wood splinters out of his poor legs and feet, and sponging 'em off as gentle as I knew how.

It seemed like we'd been at it for hours, the doc and I, when Virge groaned, and his eyes came open, and he saw me. I didn't say a word, just looked back at him, my heart pouring out all the love that was in me and hoping he'd understand. I reckon he did, 'cause he tried to smile—and seeing that I nearly broke down. Then he whispered: "They haven't got me yet."

"Nor will as long as I've got breath." It was a promise.

He went unconscious again, but told me later he knew I was there, fighting with him, and the thought of leaving me gave him strength. That's how it was with us always, like we was joined, each taking from the other what was needed, and neither of us holding back. Not ever.

It was a long time before he was on his feet, though, and I was wore out, but never said it. The only good thing about those months was that my sister Lydia's daughter, Josephine, and her husband had come to live with us. Lydia, Melissa, and I had kept in touch over all the years, and Josephine's husband was a mining man who'd come out West to try his hand at getting lucky. He never did, but we was lucky having 'em—and their daughter Hildreth, who I helped birth right there in our house.

She was a bright-eyed, happy little thing and just what Virge needed to help pass his days. He was sitting up by then, and getting around on a crutch, but it wasn't what he was used to, and he hated having to ask for help and being stuck in the house. But that baby gave him the most pleasure! He'd sit, holding her for hours, tickling her little toes and bouncing her, then letting her fall asleep in his lap. Seeing him gone all soft and gentle always gave me a pang when I thought of the kids we could've had and didn't.

Well, I'll say it again. Our life wasn't one fit for kids, and, if I did wrong, I had good reason. It's only looking back makes me think I was foolish—too late to do anything about it. Regrets? I got plenty, but I ain't crying over 'em. I got no more tears left.

Virge got a real kick out of trying to teach Hildreth to talk. Every time she'd say her name, it came out different, and one afternoon I found him laughing his head off.

"She says her name's Hickie," he told me. "I can't get her to say it right."

So Hickie she was, then and now, although looking at her these days it's hard to see the little kid sitting on Virge's lap with her thumb in her mouth and mumbling nonsense. That's always the trouble. Kids grow up.

But we had another surprise coming, one that lit Virge up from the inside like he'd swallowed a candle. A letter came from Oregon from a girl calling herself Jane Rysdam, and she turned out to be Virge's daughter. He and her mother Ellen had got married back in Iowa, and then Virge went off to war. When he got back, she and her folks was gone, and he was told she was dead, so he never thought much about it again, and never even told me.

"You was married? All this time, you been married?" I couldn't get it through my head. In that minute he seemed like some stranger I'd been living with—the one I'd had doubts about riding on that long-ago stagecoach.

Hearing me, the light in his eyes went out. "Yeah. I was. But Pa said she died, so that was the end of it."

"How come he told you that? How come he lied? All these years . . . ?" I couldn't say any more for thinking.

"I don't know. Maybe he wasn't happy about us gettin' hitched. We were just kids, and we ran off and got married. Come to think of it, I'm not sure what was in our heads.

Like I said, we were young, and she was Dutch. Pa never cared for the Dutch."

I was still taking it in—him being married to both of us. After a minute I said: "Looks to me like you ain't much different from them Mormons. Maybe we oughta move to Utah." It came out bitter, kind of like I felt, and it hit him hard.

He hitched himself out of his chair, moving slow, and came to me. "You're the only one I want. I made my mistakes, lots of 'em. There's things I never told anybody and I'm not goin' to start. I never told you about her because I was afraid of losin' you. You're the one who makes my life worth livin', the only one since I saw you back in Council Bluffs, and that's the truth of it."

It was how he looked, standing there on his crutch, his hurt twisting his face, that tore me apart. There wasn't no doubt in me, and never was again. I put my arms around him and buried my face in his chest. Mine, I remember thinking. He's mine. That's when I told him I was stuck to him like a tick on a dog's belly, and thank the good Lord. We had a laugh over that, and the world came right again.

Of course, he was all set to hightail it off to Oregon to see this daughter of his, and his wife, who'd gone and remarried, but he was still hobbling around and suffering from headaches.

"You ain't goin' till I say you can," I told him. "You lived this long without her, you can wait a couple months. I'm not havin' you go up there and get sick, and that woman nursin' you. How'd you think I'd feel if that happened?"

"Damn it, Allie!" He thumped his fist on the chair, and I knew he was mad as hell at himself and his own body. "I'm not made right for doin' nothing, and you know it. Besides, you could go with me."

I shook my head. "It ain't right. She'd feel funny, and so would I, both of us havin' been with you."

He thought that over. "I sure got myself in a fix. But I got a daughter. Imagine that!"

"And you can go see her soon as you don't need those crutches."

Well, sometime that winter we got a letter saying that Jane was real sick, close to dying, and nothing could keep Virge home after that. I couldn't blame him. As it happened, she didn't die, and she and her new pa had a good visit. He wrote me regular, and, when he came home, I saw right off that the trip had done him good, and he was almost his old self.

But all those bones that was broken in his feet never did heal right, and for the rest of his life he walked with a limp. I didn't care. He'd come through hell, and me with him, but we was alive and closer than ever.

Chapter Thirty-Four

For a long time Virge and me had been talking about getting ourselves a little ranch. I never had much hope of doing it—a ranch meant you had to stay put and not go wandering off to wherever the next gold mine was found. But after his accident, we did just that, taking a homestead in the Kirkland Valley. We ran a few head of cattle, and I had me a flock of chickens and a little garden, even had a Mexican to help out with the heavy chores, as Virge never really got back all his strength. There was times when I knew he was hurting, but he never complained, not once, and I was careful not to let him see how much of the load I was carrying.

During that time he was asked to run for sheriff, and he did. It was a paying job, and ranching didn't bring in much, although we never went hungry.

But one day he said: "Allie, I just can't do it. I'm not up to that kind of work any more. Not in a county big as this one, anyway."

That was as close as he ever came to admitting how poorly he felt most of the time, and all I said was: "You done enough. I'd like it if you stayed home a while."

The next time he left was without me. Another of the Earp boys had had bad luck. Warren had got himself killed in Willcox, and Virge went over as soon as he heard. Warren had already been buried and a hearing held. The killer was discharged and had blown the country. It was no joke to think about how maybe Warren's brothers might show up and want an interview. Virge looked over the record of the hearing and talked to enough people to make the community nervous.

When he came back, he said: "It looks to me like Warren got what he was askin' for. He was drunk and tried to bully the fella that killed him one time too many. Warren always thought he was Wyatt, and tried to talk the guy into handin' over his pistol, but he never had the *eye* like me and Wyatt. Besides, anyone that knew the three of us knew me or Wyatt would have just jugged them if they passed over a gun, but Warren might have beat them half to death with their own gun."

But that wasn't the end of it. Wyatt came back from Alaska the next year and wanted to go over and look into that business again. He knew Virge was too damned good-natured. So they traipsed back, and I'll bet this time they really made the place nervous. Those folks remembered all too damned well how Wyatt had evened the score when Morg was killed. And if Warren had been a family favorite like Morg, I'll wager Wyatt would have killed the fella that did it whether his kid brother was asking for it or not. He wasn't Virge, and there was a few to say that someone put a knife in Warren's hand after he was shot, but everyone said he wasn't armed at all, the damned fool. Warren had rode the trail with Wyatt when they took out after Morg's killers, and they got a lot closer than they was before Morg was killed.

Anyway, that was the end of that and neither one ever told me what happened for sure. Maybe they did croak

240

somebody. They was gone long enough. One time Sadie asked Virge about it and all he told her was to have a beer. She asked me, too, not wanting to think that Wyatt had gone back to being a killer. Hell, he never quit. He'd've killed to the day he died if somebody pushed him. Some dummy who Virge hardly knew pushed him a little too hard to talk about Tombstone, and he finally fetched him up a lick one side the head with a chunk of stove wood. Anyhow, about Warren, I didn't give Sadie a damned bit of satisfaction and got a kick out of it. I told her: "You know the Earp boys."

Well, I had this dream about us living to old age on our own place. But it wasn't to be. Wyatt and Sadie came back from Alaska pretty well off. Of course, that wasn't enough for either of 'em. They wasn't ever content with what they had, was always looking to make a bigger pile some place else, sort of like believing in the pot of gold at the end of a rainbow.

It riled me that Virge had some of that in him, and, when Wyatt and Sadie started talking about going to Tonopah, and then to Goldfield, I had my say, not that it did much good.

"You ain't ever goin' into a mine again, Virge Earp. I won't stand for it. I can't. I've seen you dyin' in front of my eyes three times, and that's three times too many to suit me. You let Wyatt go and get in trouble, and Sadie with him. She's as bad as the rest of you."

"Now Allie. . . ." Virge was pulling on his mustache like he did when he was doubtful.

"And don't think you can sweet-talk me. Not this time."

He took my chin in his good hand and made me look at him. "I bet I can."

Oh, what a way with him that man had! But I was determined. "❚❚❚ damn you, Virge, let go of me!"

He gave me a smile. "Nope. You promised me where I went, you'd go. You going back on your word? Or maybe getting tired of your old man?"

That got to me—that he'd even think such a thing. "I'm not, and you know it."

"Prove it." His eyes was shining, but I wasn't about to give in.

"Make me!"

Maybe if I'd stood my ground, there and then, we'd have had a few more years, but he could get under my skin quicker than I could blink, and that's part of the reason I loved him. So we sold out, and in a couple months was in Goldfield, another god-forsaken mining town in the desert, and no better than any of the rest. Virge got offered a job as deputy sheriff, so there was money to live on, but all along I had a bad feeling. Nothing I could point to, just an itch I couldn't scratch. And when he took sick with some kind of pneumonia that was going through town, I nursed him night and day till he got better.

Then I said: "Let's leave. This place ain't healthy."

"We'll hang on a while yet."

All that summer he was in and out of bed. Whether it was the pneumonia, or his old wounds bothering him, or both, leaving was out of the question. So we hung on—and hung on—me feeling desperate and damned alone with only my fears for company.

The end came quick. You think you're ready for it, but nobody's ever ready for death. You think it'll pass you by, but it's there, waiting for its moment, and be damned to you. Along in November Virge had got so bad he went to the hospital, and I made a pest of myself, standing over him, making sure he was taking his medicine and had whatever he wanted.

That afternoon he was sitting up, reading a letter from Hickie and laughing a little, and, when I came in, he said: "Get me a cigar."

That got my hopes up. He hadn't wanted a smoke since he'd got sick. I gave him one, thinking for sure that, when he was better, we'd leave the town and the sickness and maybe go back to Colton, settle down, and be content. But it wasn't to be.

I saw the light go out of his eyes right there and then, like a candle was snuffed out, leaving the room dark. I saw it, and I knew he was gone, and nothing I could do would bring him back.

It's a terrible feeling, that minute when death comes and takes all you've got and leaves you helpless—that minute and every minute of the life that's left to you. I can't remember what I did then, and don't want to. The light had gone out of me, too, and it never came back. He was all I ever had, all I ever wanted, and with his passing it came to me that I was really homeless, 'cause wherever we'd been together had been home.

Author's Note

"Aunt Allie" Earp, as she was lovingly known to the Earp family, was the wife of Wyatt's brother, Virgil. She dictated a bona-fide memoir in reaction to a spurious earlier one done by an unscrupulous writer who she threatened to "kill" after she discovered what he had done. She was assisted by her grandniece, LaVonne Miller Griffin, who made a typescript of it at the end of each day as they went. I have had unrestricted use of this typescript in writing this book and used it as broad—and sometimes detailed—guidance, with *verbatim* use of some of it, but most conversations and situations have been amplified to heighten reader interest and understanding that is the artistic license granted to a novelist. My story was also amplified by independent research into many other sources.

Access to the above memoir was possible due to the lifelong friendship of my husband Glenn Boyer with LaVonne Griffin and her parents, Estelle and Bill Miller. Estelle was the daughter of the Earp brothers' sister, Adelia Earp Edwards. Bill Miller became the hunting companion of Wyatt for almost a quarter of a century and was the son the old frontiersman had always wanted. Glenn, in turn, was treated as a son by Bill and Estelle, which is evident in his many letters from them over the years.

Glenn was given the "Aunt Allie" memoir by LaVonne Griffin shortly before her death.

About the Author

Born and raised near Pittsburgh, Pennsylvania, Jane Candia Coleman majored in creative writing at the University of Pittsburgh but stopped writing after graduation in 1960 because she knew she "hadn't lived enough, thought enough, to write anything of interest." Her life changed dramatically when she abandoned the East for the West in 1986, and her creativity came truly into its own. *The Voices of Doves* (1988) was written soon after she moved to Tucson. It was followed by a book of poetry, *No Roof But Sky* (1990). Her short story, "Lou" in *Louis L'Amour Western Magazine* (3/94), won the Spur Award from the Western Writers of America as did her later short story, "Are You Coming Back, Phin Montana?" in *Louis L'Amour Magazine* (1/96). She has also won three Western Heritage Awards from the National Cowboy Hall of Fame. *Doc Holliday's Woman* (1995) was her first novel and one of vivid and extraordinary power. The highly acclaimed *Moving On: Stories of the West* was her first Five Star Western, and it contains her two Spur award-winning stories. It was followed in 1998 with the novel, *I, Pearl Hart*, and then her novel, *The O'Keefe Empire* (Five Star Westerns, 1999). Other story collections include *Borderlands* (Five Star Westerns, 2000) and *Country Music* (Five Star Westerns, 2002). It can be said that a story by Jane Candia Coleman embodies the essence of what is finest in the Western story, intimations of hope, vulnerability, and courage, while she plummets to the depths of her characters, conjuring moods and imagery with the consummate artistry of an accomplished poet. Her next Five Star Western will be *Lost Mesa*.